D1519050

# A
# LEAN
# YEAR
# AND
# OTHER
# STORIES

WESTERN

LITERATURE

SERIES

ROBERT

LAXALT

# A

# LEAN

# YEAR

AND

OTHER

STORIES

University of Nevada Press ▲▲ *Reno Las Vegas London*

Western Literature Series

Series Editor: John H. Irsfeld

A list of books in the series appears
at the end of this volume.

The paper used in this book meets
the requirements of American
National Standard for Information
Sciences—Permanence of Paper for
Printed Library Materials, ANSI
Z39.48-1984. Binding materials
were selected for strength and
durability.

"Old Button" first appeared in
*Nevada: Official Bicentennial Book*
(Las Vegas: Nevada Publications,
1976). Copyright © 1976 by Robert
Laxalt. Used by permission.

Library of Congress
Cataloging-in-Publication Data
Laxalt, Robert, 1923–
    A lean year and other stories /
Robert Laxalt.
        p.   cm. — (Western literature
series)
    ISBN 0-87417-241-1 (alk. paper)
    1. Nevada—Fiction. I. Title.
II. Series.
PS3562.A9525L43    1994
813'.54—dc20                93-33529
                                    CIP

University of Nevada Press, Reno,
Nevada 89557 USA
Design by Richard Hendel
Printed in the United States
of America
9  8  7  6  5  4  3  2  1

*For Nicholas Cady*

# CONTENTS

# AUTHOR'S

## NOTE

The manner in which these early writings came to light was a little bizarre.

Tom Radko, director of the University of Nevada Press, asked me if I had any short stories lying around. The story would be for an anthology that author/editor Gerald Haslam was putting together.

I thought and said, "There's one about an old buckaroo I think I can track down." I did, and that was the rebirth of "Old Button," which is included in this collection.

After reading "Old Button," Tom Radko asked if there were other short stories he could look at. I thought again and told him I wasn't sure. From time to time, writers do empty the storehouse and I couldn't remember what was saved and what was thrown out.

Nonfiction articles surfaced easily. Journalistic experience made article writing fairly painless, and that meant extra money to supplement the modest salaries of a newspaperman and his schoolteacher wife.

My first novel, "The Beginning of Desolation," and a novella rewrite, "Rimrock," also came to light. So did the revelation that New American Library had wanted to publish the latter. I had refused, saying that such asked-for changes as rustling a slow-moving band of two thousand sheep just couldn't happen in a range sheep outfit. Later I was chagrined at my impudence and ignorance, but there had been no novelists around from whom I could learn the art of the trade.

Along with a few dozen historical vignettes, I also found some twenty-five short stories that had survived. Some had been published in magazines, others of a serious bent had run headlong into the taboo-ridden barrier of popular pulp magazines and were returned with such comments as "snakes are practically automatically out."

One letter, however, was compassionate and honest. It was written by Frederic Birmingham, editor of *Esquire*.

This letter said in part: "I am afraid that you have repeated yourself in moiling about in topics which tend to be effective as literary tour de force, but almost impossible to think of in a commercial sense. . . . THE SNAKE PEN is a damn good story, . . . but my candid opinion is that you must turn your talents to more digestible backgrounds if you would succeed financially in your writing."

Out of these stories came the sixteen included in this book. They all have to do with the Nevada of the early 1950s, when I was in my late twenties.

Rummaging through the storehouse and reading stories I could only dimly remember writing made me realize how fortunate I had been in experiencing things I knew well enough to write about.

Ours had been a livestock family, so I knew ranching people. I had grown up in Carson City, so I knew life in a small town. I had gone to school from first grade on with Indian kids, and later became the first and only white fighter on the Stewart Indian School boxing team. I knew how thin the veneer of white man's civilization was, and armed with that and an actual happening I could understand and write "Sixty Miles Is a Long Trip."

Becoming a reporter and later a United Press correspondent opened the door to a treasure trove of experiences: gambling clubs and dealers, politicians, prisons, murderers, and more lethal gas executions than I want to remember. And I had been around to witness the coming of poets and artists and Old West types to Virginia City.

Going through that maze of writing revealed just how often I had tried my hand at stories serious, humorous, satirical, fantastic, and even cowboy western—which had brought me much uncomplicated writing delight.

But the most important something of value my search yielded was the Nevada I knew when it was younger. It is a Nevada that does not exist anymore, except in remote little pockets, and in memory.

September 1993

# A
## LEAN
### YEAR

"A damn sight more comfortin' than beef, and lighter, too," muttered Clint Hamilton with a small smile of self-amusement. He inserted the check into the wide leather wallet that opened like a book, his raw rough hands rumpling an edge, and shoved the wallet into the pocket of his denim jumper.

He stood alone on the platform that led from the stockyard office. Below him, the old truck stood empty. The sun was low in the sky, so that the corrals and the buildings about him were framed with a crystal light that was not as clear as it should be. In the near distance, he could see why. A haze, leaden and gray, seemed to hang like a low cloud over Reno.

"Getting more like a big city every day," Clint thought. "And that cloud is getting bigger." But it would be a long time before it stretched as far as Washoe Valley and his plot of earth, though people said that some day Reno would be that big.

"Goddam city," he muttered. "Eating its way right into ranching country."

He stretched once on the platform, clasping his fingers behind his neck and twisting the trunk of his tall body back and forth. He lifted the wide-brimmed hat that was crushed into a V in front, yawned with a wide, open-mouthed grimace, and clumped down the steps to the truck. He felt its change immediately. The heavy lethargic rumble of the rack had disappeared with the steers, and now the truck seemed to bounce as though it were weightless.

Steering onto the main highway, he entered beneath the hazy gray blanket and moved back over the route through Reno. At the stoplight, he dug two long fingers of one hand into the pocket of his Levi's and looked at his watch. Nine o'clock. An hour to kill before the bank opened. He decided to get the truck greased. God knows, it was months since it had been. When the light changed, he rumbled into a service station and stopped. He waited, but no one came over. Opening the door, he climbed out and walked across the smooth red flagstone to the lube shop. There was a car on the rack, and beneath it a short man with long arms and a cap pulled tight to his skull was pumping grease into the joints.

Clint shuffled his boots on the pavement but the man didn't turn. What the hell's the matter with him?

"Hey."

The mechanic turned and glanced at Clint resentfully. His face was sallow and flabby, and there was a grease smear on his cheek. Setting the grease gun on the rack, he walked over, wiping his hands on the rag.

"Yeah?"

"How about a lube job for my truck?"

The mechanic glanced past him at the old truck, snorted through his nose and then threw his hand in a gesture toward the two cars parked beside the shop. "Got two to go yet."

Clint looked at the little man. "That's okay," he said. "I'll wait. How long?"

The mechanic looked more resentful. "Christ, I can't tell. Hour and a half, maybe."

Clint regarded him gravely. "Okay, I'll be back." He turned and started to move away, then called back over his shoulder. "Do a good job. She needs it." Smiling to himself, he walked slowly down the street, his worn boot heels making scraping sounds on the pavement. He didn't need to turn around to see the mechanic's reaction. He could see it well enough in his mind.

He passed beneath the arch that said, "Reno. The Biggest Little City in the World," and saw only the word *City.* People lunged past him hurriedly on their way to work, and one man glanced at his worn denims and boots with a desperate envy. Christ, they're even beginning to walk fast. Getting more like city people every day.

He carefully averted his eyes from the overwhelming array of neon signs, now lifeless in daylight, that lay beyond the arch. Gambling row, like graves in the day. Quit acting like the devil's over there. You don't have to be afraid anymore. Turning his head, he set his jaw so that the corded muscles played along his cheek, and stared challengingly at the gambling clubs. A steady stream of people passed in and out of the doors. Those coming out recoiled, as if from shock, when they met the sunlight. Dumb bastards. Pockets as empty as their heads.

Clint turned away from them confidently and entered a coffee shop. Removing his wide-brimmed hat, he strode to the counter and sat down.

"Coffee," he said, and his eyes opened wide.

The waitress had already turned away, but for a second she had startled him. Although he knew instantly that he was mistaken, she had still surprised him. Looks just like Lucy. Same black hair and small face and brittle black eyes.

He watched her as she filled the cup from the coffee maker. Same build, too. Small and tight with tiny breasts that jabbed their way into the white broadcloth of her waitress getup.

Watching her, he wondered almost sentimentally what had happened to Lucy. The little bitch, he thought with a private grin of satisfaction. God, what a mean one. Best thing I ever did was to shake her. Or did she shake me? I can't remember. Anyway, she couldn't hold a candle to Ruth.

He had wondered a hundred times, and now he wondered again how two women could be so different. One as mean as the devil's daughter, and one as sweet as any damned angel. That was the way he liked to think about it himself. When the waitress set the coffee in front of him, he did not meet her eyes.

He sipped the black brew slowly, and after a moment drew a cigarette from the battered package in his jacket pocket. As he smoked, he turned his head occasionally and stared out through the grease-filmed windows at the gambling clubs across the street. It gave him a certain sense of daring to look at them, daring because Ruth had wanted him to go alone this time and he was for sure alone. A whole damned year. Didn't seem like a year, somehow.

The desolation of that last time he went home to Lucy was a little dim in his mind. There wasn't too much of it he could remember. The ride back to the valley in the first light, with the willows and fence posts and haystacks frosted hoary with pogonip, the coat with the sheepskin collar pulled high around his neck, the habit of walking too noisily over the hollow boards of the old porch and into the kitchen, lighted by a single hanging bulb, hot as fury but good to cold hands and face—and Lucy there waiting for him.

She hadn't said anything for a long time, but sat there by the kitchen table, her black eyes glittering as she watched him weave uncertainly in the doorway, the remorse like a cold ghost in his insides, wanting to tell her how sorry he was, wanting her to know somehow that he couldn't tell her, that his kind of man couldn't speak of sorrow.

"Drunk?"

He hadn't said anything, just nodded his head foolishly, he thought even then. She got to her feet and walked over to him, her tight little body jerking hard with each step. Her nostrils were pinched white.

"Ya gamble?"

After a minute, he nodded again. It was funny, but the remorse had dimmed even then, watching her like that. She stood before him, her black hair tied behind her head, her black eyes hot, looking up at him.

"How much money we got left?"

When she asked that, the remorse had returned for a terrible second. None. The money was all gone. He couldn't say anything and only looked at her out of red-rimmed eyes, and she knew.

"You no good son of a bitch!" And she had coiled that tight little body and let fly at him with her hand. But she had to stand on tiptoe to hit him, and even then the slap only glanced off his chin.

Finally, when it was all over and his hands were scratched raw from holding her off, he had gone to bed. By that time, he had been plenty mad himself, and feeling mad felt good. Damned good. The remorse in his stomach had vanished with the first slap.

The next day, Lucy had left. But he told himself he didn't give a hoot in hell. And then he had found Ruth, Ruth with the gentle eyes, who understood him, who never cussed him out, and he had almost forgotten Lucy ever lived.

Thinking of Ruth, he thought of the check: three thousand bucks. Not bad for raising a handful of weaner calves. But you didn't do it yourself. Don't think that. Remember when that scary buckskin flopped on the ice and left you lying with a broken leg? You in the warm house and Ruth out there in the deep snow with your canvas gloves big on her hands, her denims soaked through with wet, her breath blowing frosted into the cold, pitching hay to those calves? Then, changing clothes and trekking down the snowed roads to the little schoolhouse and teaching the ranch kids there all day? Never a word of complaint. Don't forget that. Don't ever forget that.

The coffee was done and he stubbed the cigarette out in the saucer. Rising, he jammed one hand into the tight pocket of his pants and came up with a silver dollar and a few wisps of hay. Another waitress gave him his change and he looked for the little one. She was filling another coffee cup.

Outside, he looked at his watch again. Nine-thirty. Another hour to kill. He looked at the gambling clubs again. Look at them all you want. You don't need to be afraid anymore.

Just to show he wasn't afraid, he crossed the street and stood in front of them. Whenever the doors opened, he could hear the clanking of the slot machines and the voices of the croupiers at the tables. He listened for a moment, breathing heavily. Then he entered through one of the swinging doors. A look never hurt anyone.

For a moment, all the noise and talking confused him. He stepped to one side and looked at the hall. On both sides of the entrance stood an army of slot machines, cold and regimental in unerring rows, grinding and clanking, grinding and clanking, the people that stood before them shoving in their money, pulling the handles, grinding and clanking. Don't they know it's day outside?

A bouncer with red silk cowboy shirt and green-stamped boots walked past and eyed him, then walked on. Clint pulled the denim jumper down as though trying to make it cover the length of his faded Levi's, then moved toward the bar. Be out of the way there.

But even the bar was crowded, though it was morning, and he passed down its length and found an empty stool at one end. It seemed as though the bartender had been waiting for him, with his pink face and brimming blue eyes and stiff white barcoat.

"What'll it be?" His voice was like his face, bubbling.

"Beer," Clint started to say, then changed it. "Ditch."

He placed a half-dollar on the bar. The bartender didn't touch it. "Sixty," he said. Clint dug down into his pocket and put a quarter beside the half-dollar. Don't they ever stop going up?

He sipped the drink and looked at the mirror behind the bar to watch the gambling tables. It made the people and the money softer, somehow, watching them in a mirror. It gave everything a deeper quality, gave everything a sheen that was pleasing to see. But that was the trouble. It wasn't real. He turned sideways on the stool and looked about.

It was all the same. Nothing had changed, really, in a year. Maybe the dealers, but he couldn't remember that. You never see the people on the business end when you're gambling.

The dice tables, the twenty-one tables, the roulette tables were all lined in a great oval inside the hall, like a ring of soft green felt, inviting, dull shining stacks of silver dollars, and gleaming roulette wheels that whirred with the sound of spinning ivory balls. Inside the oval were the dealers and the croupiers, men with wine and blue shirts at the roulette and dice tables, and women with green silk cowboy shirts dealing twenty-one. Through their ranks, peering incessantly about, but not at the customers, roved the pit boss. Money. Can't even trust the people you work with.

Yet the sight of all the stacks of silver dollars didn't arouse anything in Clint. It never had. It was too overwhelming. The only thing you worry about when you're gambling is the money right in front of you.

Around the great oval stood the customers, staring blankly, faces heavy, mouths down at the corners, looking at their hands or watching the spin of the ivory ball on the roulette wheel, or the crazy hopping of the dice. In spite of all the people in the hall, the voice hum was barely audible, and then it was flat and hard. No one laughs in a gambling joint. This is business. Serious business.

Clint turned away again and gulped at his drink. The barstool seemed uncomfortable and he rose to his feet and leaned on one elbow. Through the mirror, he saw a man leave the twenty-one table behind him. Clint looked down quickly at his drink. He stared at it for a while and tried to listen to the conversation of the two men beside him.

"What're you gonna tell her?"

"I dunno." The man's voice was hoarse and tired and smoked out.

"What did you tell her last time?"

"Thought I'd try something different. It was morning and I walked into the kitchen straight as hell, set down at the table and said, 'Where's my breakfast?'"

"What'd she do?"

"Threw me out."

Clint raised his glass and gulped it empty. He looked into the mirror. The place at the twenty-one table was still empty. It was like a missing tooth in a grinning mouth. What the hell? What's a buck, or so?

He shoved the glass away and crossed to the table. Another man was headed there too, and for an instant Clint faltered, then stepped quickly into the gap. The other man drew up short and veered off.

Clint opened the button on his jacket pocket and took out the wallet. There was a five-dollar bill with the check. He took it out, shoved the wallet back into his pocket, and moved the bill towards the dealer.

"Dollars or halves?"

He drew in his breath sharply. Brittle black eyes and black hair and tight body. God, again like Lucy. What's the matter?

"Dollars or halves?" she repeated. Her voice was like the money she handled. Metallic.

"Halves."

He took the stack of half-dollars and shoved one on the bet spot. The cards flashed around, darting like snakes out of the small, white hands. He picked up his hand. Twelve. He scratched for a hit. An eight. Twenty. He laid his hand down on the green felt, face down, and placed the half-dollar on it.

She flipped over her hole card. Fifteen. Have to hit. She faced another card and placed it on her hand. An eight. Bust. She flipped a dollar to the man next to Clint and a half-dollar to him. He let both half-dollars stay on the bet spot. Let it ride. It's house money.

His face grew heavy and his mouth pulled down at the corners. The hum of voices and the whir of wheels faded away. He watched the cards. What the hell time is it? There's no clocks in a gambling joint.

He pulled out a watch by its short leather strap. Christ. Twelve o'clock noon. He shook his head and looked around, then reached down and scooped up the silver dollars. Must be fifty at least. He shoved them towards the girl. She whisked them into stacks of ten and gave him back four ten-dollar bills and three silver dollars. He stepped away from the table and backed up to the bar. The bartender was standing there again. He glanced at the tens in Clint's hand and bubbled, "Better than working for a living." He didn't pause, but kept right on in the same breath, "What'll it be?"

He started to say "ditch" again, but changed it. "Straight," he said. He could use a drink. He was a little bit mixed up, like waking suddenly out of a drunk sleep. He looked at the money in his hand for a minute, then slipped the bills into the wallet with the check. They filled out the leather so that the wallet was plump. You don't know the half of it, bartender. You never worked on a ranch.

The whiskey was good, hot like a poker in his throat. And when it was down, he could think clearly, think clearly enough to feel dismay. What the hell was he going to say to Ruth, even though he'd won. He couldn't tell her he'd gambled. With Lucy, yes. As long as he won, she was happy as hell. But not Ruth. He saw her gentle eyes. Eyes with hurt in them. He whimpered in his throat. She won't say anything. She'll forgive you. You know she won't say anything. But that's the trouble. Oh Jesus, what a mess! You win when you can't afford to.

He tapped the shot glass down on the bar and the bartender moved over to him.

"Same."

The bartender filled it reluctantly. "Take it easy," he said. "This stuff ain't water."

Mind your own damn business. He didn't say it aloud, but the bartender read it in the hotness that had come into his eyes. He took Clint's money and turned around, his lips twisted in barely noticeable disdain. That's what you get when you try and help them.

Clint downed the shot at one gulp, not even bothering to sip. He looked in the mirror. The place at the table was still empty. Slowly and deliberately, as though he were being driven, he walked to the gap and pulled the wallet out of his jacket pocket. What else can you do except try to lose it. He fingered the folds and pulled out the bills, then laid one on the bet spot. The little black-eyed dealer lifted an eyebrow at him, but no one else even looked.

It seemed as though he'd been there only a minute, when he was stepping back again. And this time even the silver in his pocket was gone. Okay, it was all back where it came from. You're cleaner than when you came in, and nothing to worry about. But there was an anger burning like a brand in his stomach. He'd thrown it away. Good money. Thrown it away by hitting on anything. It was enough to make a man sick, to gamble like that.

He searched for some change. He really wanted a drink now. He needed one to shake the sickness in him. But God, there wasn't even that much change left. Something white loomed beside him and he saw that the bartender was standing there again. The twist was still on his lips. Clint didn't look at him. Instead, he shook his head and turned away.

"Easy come, easy go," the bartender murmured as he moved away, but loud enough so that Clint could hear, and so could the others around him. One man smiled in comradely fashion at Clint. Turn your head, you drunken bastard. I still got money in my pocket. He shoved himself away from the bar and went to the cashier's window. What the hell's a buck or so? He could take cash to the bank instead of a check. Then, as though for the first time, he remembered the truck. He'd have to pay for the grease job. That was it. He could pad that a buck or two. Enough for a drink or so. And yet his fingers stiffened when he held the check out to the cashier in her little barred cell. When she took it, it felt somehow as if she had taken his arm.

The cashier inspected the check and then handed it on to a man with a white shirt and glasses and a pale face. He scrutinized it swiftly, then nodded. The cashier counted out three thousand dollars in hundred-dollar bills. The man at the bar who had smiled in comradely fashion stared with eyes bugged out as Clint returned, stuffing the thick wad of bills into the wallet. The bartender looked startled as Clint flipped one of the hundreds onto the bar. Take a good look, you bastard.

He downed three more shots in quick succession, until finally the whiskey only seemed warm in his stomach. He could feel a flush rising to his face and the tension ease out of his limbs. He drank and looked at the bartender and smiled. It was easy to smile with a twist to his lips. The bartender looked worn, as if someone had played a cruel joke on him.

When the third drink was gone, Clint tapped his glass on the bar for another. You know you don't have to make that much noise. Yeah, but so does he. So does the bartender. That's the difference.

All the bubble was gone from the bartender's face when he filled up the shot glass. His face was grim so that he didn't even smile at the other customers down the bar. Clint picked up the drink and sauntered to the gambling table. He knew the bartender was watching him as he walked.

It happened before he really knew it had. It had all seemed to be part of that, of putting the lousy bartender in his place. Cashing the check. Flashing the roll. Buying the shots. And last of all, plunking a twenty down on the bet spot. He came to only when the girl had faced her hand. Blackjack. And gathered in his money.

He drew in his breath sharply in surprise, so that the girl looked at him curiously out of her black eyes. For an instant he imagined he had reeled in his tracks. The twenty was gone. Twenty out of his check. Gone. He couldn't explain his way out of that. He had a sudden vision of gentle gray eyes. A thin warning shaft of cold pierced his stomach.

The girl broke the deck, shuffled, broke again, and shuffled again. Then she buried the top card under and started dealing. When she came to Clint, she turned and looked at him questioningly. His bet spot was empty. He looked at the change out of the hundred-dollar bill for a long moment, and then, as though he were touching fire, he jerked another twenty out of the roll and placed it on the bet spot. You can't do anything else. You got to get that money back. But it never comes back. Not when you want it the way you do.

It was a half hour before he realized that the shot glass was still full of whiskey. He looked at it detachedly, then lifted it to his lips. He lowered the glass with a grimace. The whiskey had grown warm.

Now, the wallet was down on the green felt. He looked at the worn leather in fascination. What the hell time is it? Forget about the time now. You got to get that money back. But how much to go now. Three hundred. Oh Christ, I'll never make it. Oh God, please help me. Does anyone pray at a gambling table?

Once, when the girl leaned forward to collect his money again, she murmured in a low voice, "Go home, cowboy. Go home before you're broke."

He glanced at her with supplication, as though she could help him fight the way back. Then he realized she was no more of a master over the way the cards fell than he, that they were both hapless viewers of the falling of the cards. He stared at her defiantly. Mind your own damned business.

The hand that probed into the pocket of the wallet found nothing. The fingers groped spasmodically into the leather folds and knew that there was nothing there. He pushed himself away from the table and almost tottered to the bar. He stared at the table with widened eyes, for a long time, then sank onto the stool and stared again. Then he stared at the floor.

Behind him, the bartender watched. And as he watched, the satisfaction faded from his face. How many times? Oh, my God, how many times? He filled a shot glass and set it down beside Clint.

Clint turned his head when the bartender touched his elbow. He looked down at the glass and then seemed to be entranced by the shining liquid. Finally, he raised his eyes and shook his head. Rising to his feet, he propelled himself forward and out of the gambling club. He heard nothing when he passed the clanking army that lined the approaches to the door.

The pavement was hot with the heat of autumn afternoon, but he did not notice it. He strode down its length swiftly and was unnoticeable in the fast-moving sidewalk throng. There was a driven fury to his movements, as though he were bent upon a goal. Finally, he noticed it and could not remember what the goal was. The Reno arch passed above him but he saw none of the words.

Then he was walking uncertainly across the smooth red stone

that surrounded the service station. The truck stood waiting beside the grease rack. As he paused in back of it, the attendant emerged from the lube shop, a bill in his hand. His sallow brow was beaded with sweat.

"Four bucks, mister."

Clint made a motion as if to reach for his wallet. Then he let his hand drop to his side. Almost imperceptibly, his shoulders slumped so that he appeared to be carrying a weight that crushed him downwards. He glanced evasively toward the attendant, then at the truck as he spoke.

"Gonna have to ask you to charge it to me. I'll catch you up on my next trip into town." He closed his eyes for a brief instant.

The attendant was silent. "Sorry, mister. We don't carry charge accounts here." God, am I going to enjoy this.

"But . . ." Clint stopped and groped. There was nothing to say. You're beat. You've got to beg. And men like you aren't meant to beg.

Suddenly, he thought of the gun. It was in the jockey box. He could leave the gun as security. Better yet, he could hock it and pay the bill. There would be money left over. He could try again. He would win that money back yet. His shoulders straightened and he raised his head. Then, like a stunning blow that traveled through the gray fog, he remembered. The gun wasn't in the jockey box. He had moved it to the bureau drawer in the bedroom. He cast one unseeing, helpless glance at the attendant and then dropped his head.

The attendant winced and a deep hurt came into his eyes. There was a silence and then he spoke softly. "Okay, cowboy. Just give me your address and I'll send you a bill."

Clint mumbled out the address. He could not look at the attendant. You rotten bastard. You didn't have to say it like that. God, what a bastard you are.

The cab of the truck was like a furnace, but he started the engine before he rolled down the windows. Under the denim jacket, he could feel the sweat trickling wet from his armpits. He backed the truck out and moved into the line of traffic.

He drove slowly out on the highway that led south from Reno.

Houses and stores began to give way to green fields and long fence lines. When he turned his head, he could see the desert mountains to the east. Range upon range they lay, barren and gray and hungry in the heat of the autumn sun. Don't look at them. No one looks at the desert hills until winter. Turn your head the other way and look at the Sierra, high and young and green, and not hungry for you. But you can't see them now. Not this trip, anyway. He passed a stock corral that lay next to the road. There was a cow sitting on a huge dunghill: God and his world.

The truck slowed as he climbed the small ridge that divided the two valleys, then gained momentum as he sped downhill into the wide expanse of green fields, fields that shimmered now in a pool of autumn sun. Occasionally, a puff of warm air blew against his face. In the near distance he could see the schoolhouse. He slowed the truck and turned off onto the dirt road, but the school-yard was empty of bikes and sound. Ruth would be home. A sliver of cold pricked his insides. Oh, God, it's beginning. But it hasn't been gone. The seed has been there all the time.

The Sierra loomed before him, higher it seemed than he had ever seen it. And when he glanced at the rear-view mirror, he saw that he was leaving a long winding cloud in his wake. He looked ahead and saw the thin waft of smoke climbing from the chimney. The ranch was before him.

He steered the truck through the open gate and pulled to a stop beside the faded brown boards of the house. But after he had turned off the engine and set the emergency brake, he sat motion-less for a long while, staring at the stalls where the steers had been raised. They were empty and still. A shiver shook his frame.

Finally, he climbed out and mounted the three steps to the old wooden porch. The kitchen door was open, but he could see noth-ing through the screen. He walked quietly over the old boards.

Pulling open the screen door, he stepped inside and took off his hat. His hair was pasted wet to his forehead, and his face was white. Ruth was standing by the stove and turned when he en-tered. But she must have heard the truck. She knew I was here.

He stood unmoving inside the doorway. Help me, Ruth. Please help me. Help me for all the things I can't say.

She spoke first, softly. "You've been gone a long time."

He did not answer. He could not even nod his head.

She turned briefly to him, but not so that he could see her eyes, and said, "Dinner's almost ready. Do you want to wash?"

Clint felt his defenses breaking inside of him. There was an expression of fright on his face, as though this was how he had expected it would be. He swayed once and then jerked himself to with an effort and stalked toward her. "It's gone," he whispered hoarsely. "Every damned penny is gone."

She was arranging the knife and fork beside his plate. When she did not answer, he grasped her wrist fiercely and jerked her about like a doll. "Say something," he cried. "Say something, damn you!"

He saw her eyes then, not resigned, or vengeful, but gray and gentle and dull with hurt. His face twisted in pain. "What're you doing to me?" he almost shouted. No, not that. Please don't say it. Please don't say it.

"It's all right, Clint," she said. "All it means is a lean year. Can't you see that?"

He felt as though he had died. His shoulders slumped, and for an instant he thought he would fall. He rocked unsteadily and then turned his body and drove himself toward the bedroom door. When he had passed through, he closed it quietly behind him. The print spread was fixed neatly on the bed and the room was cool. He stumbled forward and fell prone across the bed.

For many long moments, he lay with his face pressed into the spread. Then, slowly, he turned his head and stared across the room at the bureau drawer.

"Oh God, Lucy. I miss you so."

# OLD

## BUTTON

There was a faraway moan in the wind, so muted and faint that it seemed almost to come from another world. Night had followed swiftly on the heels of the storm, and the corners of the bunkhouse were already thick with darkness, obscuring all but the worn, shining pommel of a saddle, a silver crusted bit on a bridle, and the dull gleam of a carbine on the wall. They listened to the moan in the wind and the rustling of the wood in the stove, and wished that Buzz would come quickly.

Frisco Jack turned his fixed gaze away from the red chinks in the stove and stared at the figure on the cot. His eyes narrowed as he saw grayness in the old face and the gnarled hands. There was a rustle of canvas from the cot and they knew he was awake. Frisco Jack rose swiftly and leaned over him, and even Henry, the Indian buckaroo, shifted in his chair and inclined his head toward the cot.

"Do it feel better now?" asked Frisco Jack.

When there was no answer, Frisco Jack groaned, "I'm sorry, Old Button. It was all my doing, me and my big mouth."

The voice from the cot was half gasp, half whisper. "It weren't your doing. It weren't your doing at all. It was that saddle. If it hadn't slipped, I wouldn't of been thrown at all."

Frisco Jack glanced at Henry, hoping he would say nothing. But there was no need to worry. In the red light from the stove, the old Indian's face was as silent and impassive as rock.

Old Button turned his head to look at Henry. "Who's there? Who's that there?" He squinted his eyes and peered into the darkness. "What the hell you doing here, black old Winnemucca?"

Henry said nothing, but there was a warm light of a smile in his black eyes at the familiar banter. He sat back in his chair and continued to stare silently at Old Button.

A gust of cold air cut like a knife through the warmth of the bunkhouse when Buzz opened the door. He did not even bother to shake the snow from his hat and coat, but strode swiftly to the cot. He held Old Button's wrist in his hands for a long moment, then placed his palm flat against the tiny cage of the old man's chest.

"Is it any better, old man?" he asked. "Suzy wants to know can you take some broth?"

Old Button shook his head. "I ain't hungry, Buzz. But you thank her anyway. I'll be all right."

Frisco Jack had been watching Buzz intently, noticing the grim line of his mouth. "When's the doc coming, Buzz?" he asked.

"He can't come tonight," Buzz answered flatly. "The wind's drifted the road shut tighter than a tick. They can't clear it until morning at least."

Frisco Jack leaped to his feet. "Damn his coward hide! A little snow maybe can stop him, but it won't stop me. Give me the pickup, Buzz. I'll take Old Button through."

Buzz shook his head. "Doc says we shan't move him. And besides, it ain't a little snow. It's a big one getting bigger every minute. If it don't break come daylight, we'll be in big trouble ourselves. All that stock in the North Fork and valley both has got to be moved to high ground before they wallow down in the drifts."

Old Button's voice whispered from the cot. "Now, Jack, you take it easy. I'll be fine here until morning." He was silent for a moment, and then he added, "Ain't nothing going to happen to me tonight. I ain't made to die in bed. You know that."

Frisco Jack closed his eyes helplessly at the uncertainty in the old man's voice. "I know that, Old Button," he said. "I ain't worried about you dying in bed. When your time comes, you'll go in the saddle, just like your daddy and his daddy before him. I know that."

Buzz glanced curiously at Frisco Jack before he interrupted. "We better get up to the ranch house and get some food in us. Suzy's keeping it warm." When Frisco Jack made as if to protest, Buzz motioned him still. Then he turned and leaned over the cot. "Will you be okay for a little while, old man?"

Old Button nodded and they rose to go. Henry was the last to pass the cot. He stopped for an instant and looked down at the old face and the little hands, even grayer now, showing through the bronze of sun and wind.

Old Button's face twisted in the familiar scowl, but the words died unspoken. He stared at the Indian mutely, and as he stared, his mouth trembled.

"I'm scared, Henry," he whispered. "I ain't never gonna move from this bed again."

The Indian shook his head. "Old buckaroo never die when big work to be done. You go to sleep now. We got long day tomorrow."

They were waiting on the board stoop when Henry passed through the door, and Buzz asked him in a low voice, "He's done for, ain't he, Henry?"

When the Indian nodded slowly, Frisco Jack wheeled as if to re-enter the bunkhouse. "Then why the damned hell we leaving him?" he demanded in a tortured voice. "If he's got to die in bed, then by God, the least I can do is stay with him."

Buzz reached out and blocked the door. "It ain't decent to watch a man die, Jack. Leave him go alone."

Henry grunted in assent. "You not worry, Jack. Old Button find way alone."

Frisco Jack paused, puzzled and yet strangely comforted by Henry's words. He looked intently at the old Indian for a long moment, and then he led the others into the swirling darkness. As they crossed the yard, Buzz noted aloud with satisfaction that the heavy clouds had finally parted high overhead. The storm was breaking, and only the wind remained to play at whipping the snow about in mock fury.

Inside the bunkhouse, Old Button listened intently until the low rumble of voices faded away, then he lay back and stared into the darkness overhead. But when he realized that his eyes were closing, he rose with a start, fear gripping his heart with an icy hand.

Adjusting the pillow under his head, he peered about into the thick gloom. By the red, flickering light of the stove, he could see the hair chaps hanging from the peg on the wall.

"If I'd a worn those today," he muttered, "bet I wouldn't of been thrown so bad."

Then he had been thrown, after all. The saddle hadn't slipped. He had really been thrown, all right. Might as well face up to it, he thought. And it wasn't Frisco Jack's big mouth that was to blame for it all. It was his own.

They had all been sitting on the corral fence that afternoon, casting occasional glances at the clouds settling low and leaden from horizon to horizon, and waiting for Frisco Jack to step into the saddle.

Ordinarily, they wouldn't even have watched, but this was no ordinary horse. This was a powerful stallion caught from the wild bunch, black as midnight, with meanness shining clear through him. Frisco Jack had broken him to stand and saddle, but they all knew he would take no rider.

Even before Frisco Jack hit the saddle, the stallion took off, uncoiling like a piece of black lightning. And Frisco Jack hung on with both hands as the stallion fishtailed and snapped in two like a whip, churning up the corral dust and even ramming broadside once into the corral.

They yipped and shouted like wild men as Frisco Jack stuck it out for one pass around the corral. Then, one jarring twist jerked him off balance, another started him going, and the last heaved him into a corner.

The stallion didn't go after him, but bucked his way into another corner and stood there, his black sides heaving, his outlaw eyes rimmed with white, and his nostrils flaring like bellows. Frisco Jack picked himself up and limped to where the others sat, not even bothering to shake off the dust that covered him or feel the bloody bruise on his cheekbone. It was then that Old Button had said the wrong thing.

"Now, I ain't saying there just ain't no more buckaroos," he said aloud to no one in particular. "But I seen the day when my old Ma could ride that thing with a money piece between her boot and the stirrup."

But this time, Frisco Jack was in no mood for banter. He was skinned and shaken and mad. Instead of laughing, he pulled a silver dollar out of his pocket and flipped it angrily at Old Button.

"There's your money piece, old runny mouth," he spat out. "Let's see if you're as good a man as your Ma."

Even after Frisco Jack said it, he hadn't backed down, but stood there looking defiantly at Old Button. There was nothing else to do but pick up the dollar and start in the direction of the stallion.

It was then Buzz intervened. "Listen," he said, laughing in open amusement. "You ain't any chicken anymore. You haven't been on a bucker in ten years. That's too much horse for an old man like you."

Frisco Jack had chimed in then, grasping Old Button's sleeve and not even bothering to conceal his derision. "Who the hell you trying to kid?" he scoffed. "That ain't no old man's pony, you know."

But Old Button had shaken off Frisco Jack's hand, his face flaring with humiliation and anger, and moved for the stallion.

They knew there was no stopping him then, so they backed up to the fence and waited for it to happen, hoping he would be thrown quickly.

The stallion stood stock-still as Old Button hitched up his Levi's, rocked on his worn heels for an instant, and then placed the silver dollar on the stirrup. But Old Button wanted to make sure the stallion stayed still until he was firm in the saddle. Just before he swung his leg over, he reached up with his left hand and twisted the stallion's ear.

That old buckaroo trick got him into the saddle, all right. But that was all. On the first jump, Old Button felt something tear inside and he screamed aloud. The stallion cracked double once more, and the old man's light little body hurtled into the air and landed in the dirt like an old sack.

And so now it was done. All the little needles of hurt that old age had brought him through good-natured insults, all the little pangs that he had suffered and tried so unsuccessfully to forget, had been climaxed by the shame of this day. And he would die not like a buckaroo, not like his daddy and his daddy before him, in the saddle. But like any old man, in a bed.

He covered his eyes with his arms, and for a long while, the hard folds of the canvas shook gently, and then became still.

It had been a terrible effort. He could not remember ever having cried before. And now that it was done, he felt an overwhelming drowsiness creep over his body.

Outside, the wind was moaning again, lonely and very near. It cried about the edge of the bunkhouse and whimpered at the crack under the door. The wood in the stove whispered as it settled for the last time. Old Button heard these things and watched with a distant helplessness as the drowsiness enveloped his body and grayed out the stove, the saddle in the corner, and the hair chaps on the wall.

The bunkhouse was cold when he awoke, and the single window was framed with an uncertain light. He sat bolt upright in bed and stared about him. The canvasses on the other cots had already been pulled high, and the bunkhouse was empty. He swung his legs quickly over the side of his cot, furious that the others had not awakened him earlier.

Then he remembered, and almost gasped in pain before he realized there was no pain. Gingerly, he pressed his fingers against his abdomen. There was no pain. The terrible bleeding he had felt inside the night before was gone, completely and surely gone. He could have shouted in amazement and joy.

But there was no time for that. Outside, the wind had not diminished, but had grown wilder. It was screaming like a madman now, roaring down upon the bunkhouse and hurling great sheets of snow across the window.

He dressed hurriedly, jerking on his high boots and hoping desperately that the others had not already left after the stock. Deep inside his clothes sack, he found a warm winter shirt and heavy, fur-backed gloves. Reaching under his mattress, he pulled out the long sheepskin coat, creased and musty from many months of confinement. And from the wall, he jerked down the hair chaps.

When he opened the bunkhouse door and stepped into the yard, the flying snow leaped wet and cold into his face. He turned his head towards the storm, and moved quickly through the drifts. In all his life, he could not remember a storm so fierce. It blotted out all the world except the tiny sphere in which he walked. Its wailing filled his ears and the snow stung his face, but he welcomed it with a savage hunger.

When he clumped into the ranch house and shrugged off the sheepskin coat, he could hardly suppress a grin at the chorus of astonished yelps that greeted him.

Suzy was the first to reach him. "You shouldn't be out of bed, Button," she exclaimed. "Not until the doctor's checked you."

He waved her aside and thumped his chest and stomach with quick blows. "Why, you think that little fall would lay me up more'n one night? You don't know much about old buckaroos. Ask black Winnemucca there. He'll tell you about old buckaroos."

The Indian said nothing, but he smiled slowly when Button sat down beside him at the table.

"You sure you're okay, Button?" asked Buzz intently.

"Hell yes, he's okay," Frisco Jack answered for him. "Look at him! Tough and hard as he ever was. You can't keep that one down when there's big work to be done."

Button grinned and began to eat his breakfast quickly, so that the others would not have to wait. He attacked the sausages and the eggs and the hotcakes ravenously, gulping down the steaming coffee between mouthfuls. He could not remember when breakfast had tasted so good.

When he was done, they rose together and clumped to the door, their heels thumping hollow against the wooden floor of the kitchen. It was a good sound, boots against the floor, thought Button.

Buzz faced them as they slid into their heavy coats. "We're shorthanded, but we can't take any chances on splitting up in this storm," he said. "The most of the stock is in the North Fork. We'll ride there first and hope to blazes we can get them to high ground today. But there ain't a chance in the world of saving them steers in the valley."

"I'll ride to the valley, Buzz," said Button simply. "I know that ground like the back of my hand. I can get them beefs to high ground, and you know I can."

Buzz stared hard into Button's eyes. "I know you can, Button. If there's any man can do it, it's you."

They pulled on their wide-brimmed hats and stepped into the screaming wind and flying snow. It was inconceivable, but the storm had actually become worse. The drifts in the yard were already up to their waists.

In the dim, early morning light of the barn, they picked out the strongest horses they could find. But many minutes had passed before anyone realized what horse Button had chosen for himself. It was the black stallion.

"My God, that horse ain't broke!" exclaimed Buzz.

In answer, Button swung himself lightly into the saddle. The stallion took his weight without a tremor. He stood there, his black head raised high and his powerful barrel faintly lifting with each breath.

"Why, I guess you showed that horse yesterday," crowed Frisco Jack. "I guess that little ride broke you a horse, all right. I gotta hand it to you, Button. You're the best buckaroo ever I see."

Henry opened the barn door and they moved slowly into the drifted yard, the horses tossing their heads excitedly at the stinging flakes. At the outer gate, they grouped together for an instant in a wordless goodbye, and then they parted and went their different ways. When Button turned once in the saddle, Buzz and Frisco Jack and Henry were fading into a stormy mist. He felt a deep, sudden flow of kinship for them. Then he turned and set his jaw for the terrible job ahead.

At the last corral, Button laid his direction for the distant valley. North and south and east and west were lost in the white haze that whirled about him. It did little good to look into the face of the storm. He could see nothing, and the flakes cut like tiny daggers into the bare skin of his face. Raising his bandanna until it covered his nose, he hunched forward in the saddle and prepared to travel by instinct alone.

The black stallion seemed unaffected by the storm. His powerful legs plowed tirelessly hour after hour through the high sea of drifts. Button saw the firm white jets of steam that issued from his nostrils and felt the power between his legs, and was secure.

When they came to the creek, almost hidden now by towering banks of snow, the stallion stopped. Button lifted his boots high and flicked the reins, and the stallion stepped surely into the rushing water. Button could only marvel that a horse could be so strong. They reached the far bank and resumed their plodding pace through a world of white.

For a moment, Button could not believe his eyes. The veil of the storm was split for the briefest of instants, and there before him were the steers, bunched together in the smothering whiteness. He had never expected to find them so easily, and for an instant, he was astonished that his sense of direction could be so true. Then, vaguely, he realized that his hand had been limp to the reins for a long time before. The stallion had found the direction.

He urged the stallion forward until his forequarters jarred

against the rump of a steer. The startled animal gave one quick leap, struggled to go further, quit his plunging and turned to stare at them through snow-rimmed eyes.

Then, Button realized that the stock could never be driven to high ground. There was only one out to the dilemma, ride ahead to the foothills and bank on the almost impossible hope that the cavvy would be there. Turning the stallion, he skirted the herd and plowed toward the mountain.

Again, the stallion took his head and moved certainly forward, and when the wind suddenly began to subside, Button knew they were moving into the lee side of the foothills. When he saw the big band of horses huddled together, he yipped aloud in exultation. It was almost too much to comprehend. Again, he had found that for which he searched.

Quickly and methodically, he moved into the band and cut out some twenty horses. Uncoiling his rope, he tied the leaders together, then moved back and whipped them down into the valley. They went reluctantly, pitching and kicking. But they went, and that was the important thing.

In the hours that followed, he drove them back and forth between the valley and the foothills, pounding an ever clearer path through the drifts. But by the time he had finished prodding and thumping the steers into the beaten path, darkness was already beginning to fall.

And finally, the stallion's strength was going. He slipped and floundered often now, and the once proud head was low. His great chest heaved with shuddering breaths, and his legs were caving. Button knew that in the stallion had lain his only hope of finding his way back to the ranch. But this did not seem important somehow. A magnificent horse was dying, and Button felt a sadness that this should be.

Night had fallen black, and the slivers that pierced his face were invisible slivers. Yet, Button did not really notice. There was an overwhelming drowsiness creeping over his body, and he knew a happiness he had not known since the days of his youth. Gently, he reined the stallion into the storm and the blackness of the valley.

# SIXTY
## MILES
## IS
## A
## LONG
## TRIP

If smiling had been part of his makeup, Kominsky would have smiled. Twice during the evening he had chanced to look through the smoke-glazed window and seen O'Malia come out of his own saloon across the street and stand with his hands on his hips, watching the Indians troop into Kominsky's saloon. From that distance, Kominsky couldn't see O'Malia's lips moving, but by the bursts of vapor that frosted furiously in the night air, he knew he was swearing a streak.

Kominsky did not like full-blooded Irishmen any more than he liked Indians, else he might have been able to feel a little sympathy for him. And besides, as Kominsky often said, O'Malia had been in Nevada only ten years and therefore couldn't be expected to understand Indians. That was a lie on the face of it, though, because if you took it from a man who did know his Indians, like old Sheriff Farrell, there was no real knowing of Paiutes, ever.

But one way or another, it was a good one on O'Malia. A few years back, when the government ban on sale of liquor to Indians was being argued around in Washington, D.C., he had seen the handwriting on the wall and begun selling whiskey to the Paiutes, both under the bar and sometimes over, calculating that when the ban was lifted, he would have the Indian trade corralled. But when the ban went off and the Indians could go into saloons and drink, not one of them ever went back to O'Malia's. Instead, they moved across the street to Kominsky, who had refused to sell them a drop before.

At first, Kominsky had served the Indians with open hostility, but the first time he counted up his Saturday night receipts from the payroll of the big Con Copper Mine where most of them worked, he began to realize what O'Malia had lost. He learned something else for the first time, too: just how much a Paiute could drink. After that, he didn't mind losing the buckaroo trade. Cowboys never had much money, anyway, and they weren't the kind that settled in one saloon and drank.

The joke in town was that Kominsky had the Indian sign on the Indians, because they never made trouble in his saloon, and always waited until they were somewhere else to do that.

In a sense, this was true, but it was Kominsky's making. Even when the bar was crowded with Indians, he maintained an aloof distance, serving them what they asked for and then going back to his post in front of the cash register, to stand there with his arms crossed on his massive chest, a mountain of a man with dark, forbidding features, looking down like some malevolent god upon his own Saturday night hell of a steaming room filled with the grunting, guttural monotone of drunken, lurching Indian men and bandannaed, cackling women, and old men with cowboy hats and face dignity but not much else after the whiskey got through with them.

Distant though he was, Kominsky knew the danger signs, and

at the first murmur of trouble, he was there. All he ever needed to say was, "That's enough whiskey for you. Get out of here!" And the troublemakers went without a word. In a perverse way, this only increased Kominsky's contempt for the whole lot of them. He would have liked to see anybody throw him out of a bar, by God. Once in a while, though, some of the young Indians would pause long enough to look at him in a dead, impassive way that always managed to make a twitch of fear run along his spine. But they went, and that was the important thing, and he forgot about the moment of fear in a hurry, mostly because he couldn't understand it, and didn't want to, either.

On principle, Kominsky made it a point to learn as few names as possible of the Indians that came to his saloon. But there were a few that stuck, and one of them, a young buck they called Ivan, was at the bar now. Kominsky had reason to remember him, because he was always half drunk by the time he came in, from liquor he had bought somewhere else. And though there was nothing said about it, they both knew how much this infuriated Kominsky.

Ivan was a cut different from the rest, too. He never came in on Saturday night with his dirty clothes from the mine, but went home and changed into a buckaroo outfit, with a black scarf around his neck. He had a knife face with slit eyes and straight black eyebrows that grew together like an arrow point above his nose. Kominsky had said once in town that he bet a Mex had gotten his mother, but old Sheriff Farrell had said no, that he was supposed to look like his grandfather, who had been a war chief once.

As always he was with his older cousin, who was squat and short-armed and had gone to sloppy fat, and who followed Ivan around like a dog. He was good natured, though, and his name was Cornbread. They had come in with a white man in town, Joe Ellis, a consumptive who lived in a shack in the Indian village. Joe was bent-shouldered and meek, but in his own wheedling way, he had his pride, and he claimed the only reason he lived in the village was that he liked the Paiutes. The people in town knew different. They knew he lived in the village because the Indians didn't care whether he was consumptive as long as he had his pickup truck and they could browbeat him into taking them to Reno for a bangup time on Lake Street.

That was what the argument was about now. Once when there was a lull in the noise, Kominsky caught a snatch of it. Ivan and Cornbread had Joe Ellis between them. Ivan's sullen voice whipped across the bar. "Goddammit, old man. You said you would." And Cornbread, his voice already thick drunk, said, "Come on, Joe Ellis. We have a good time." But Joe Ellis shook his head. "I tell you, I don't feel good tonight. I didn't even want to come down here."

After that, Kominsky kept his ears open to them. He wanted only half a chance to catch Ivan making trouble. There was something about that slit-eyed young Indian that made the rage surge in his chest, and it was more than his drinking somewhere else. He would love the chance to throw him out tonight. He caught himself flexing his hands. By God, if he says one word back, I will break him in two.

The argument went on, but still in subdued mutters that he couldn't quite hear. Joe Ellis was surprisingly stubborn, his thin little mouth set and shaking his head so continuously that it looked like an affliction. In spite of his mounting anticipation, the thought crossed Kominsky's mind that he looked pretty sick at that. He was even refusing the shots that Cornbread kept urging on him.

When it happened, Kominsky was bent over the bar pouring a row of drinks. But he caught it all the same out of the corner of his eye. Ivan, his lips drawn back from his teeth like an animal, had dug his fist into Joe Ellis's side and twisted it. The little man gave a small, gasping cry that pierced through the droning swell of voices.

Kominsky had been waiting for trouble too long. It was the first time he had ever lost his restraint with the Indians. The whiskey bottle dropped from his fingers, rolled onto the tray, and then crashed to the floor in splinters. His face contorted, he lunged sideways across the bar at Ivan. One great hand missed, but the other caught Ivan by the forearm even as he was leaping back. In a flash, Ivan raised one foot to the bar, and kicked himself away. The cowboy shirt tore loose at the wrist, and Kominsky was left with the cuff grasped in his fingers.

The noise in the room cut off with the suddenness of a whiplash. But Kominsky was not hearing anything now. He bellowed once like a bull and charged down the length of the bar to the opening at the end, his swinging arms obliviously sweeping bottles and glasses to the floor as he went. When he came around the corner of the bar, there was an avenue cleared for him. At the far end of it was Ivan. But now there was a knife in his hands and he was crouched and waiting.

It was not the shine of the knife that stopped Kominsky. It was the expression on the young Indian's face. His slit eyes were wide open now and his lips were parted downward, and in his face and pose there was a terrible sort of happiness, as if something that had been strangled in him had burst its bonds and gone screaming with glee through his whole being.

Even then, Kominsky might have gone ahead with it, had not Joe Ellis stepped between them. "I don't want no trouble over me," he said.

It was such a weary plea that it was almost laughable. Yet, because it was so ineffective, it broke the tension. One of the old men grunted in assent, and after a lingering moment, several of the others followed suit. Kominsky had been hulked forward, his hands low and in front of him like a wrestler. He let them drop. "You'll go to jail for this," he said hoarsely, looking right over the top of Joe Ellis's head at Ivan.

He should have stopped there, but as soon as he began to threaten he felt his anger slipping, and with it his courage. He tried to bring it back with swearing. Everything he had ever stored up against Indians came pouring out now in garbled, disjointed epithets.

Ivan had not moved. But he did now. Throwing his head back like a coyote, he gave a shuddering yell and leaped forward, bowling little Joe Ellis aside as he went. Kominsky stepped back quickly, this time with something entirely different written on his face. But before Ivan could get to him, three big Indians stepped in front and caught his headlong rush. Two of them held him, and the third, who was his father, began to talk rapidly to him in Paiute. It filtered through, because his squirming grew less violent. Finally, his talking voice returned to him and he shouted back to his father.

The Indians let him go. He shook himself as if he were throwing something off and slipped the knife back into the sheath in his shirt. His father kept haranguing him persistently. Sniffing and jerking his head in disdain, Ivan answered him again, but this time he turned away and went towards the door. But he had not come all the way back yet, because he paused before he went out and shouted something at Kominsky, and it was in Paiute. His cousin Cornbread took Joe Ellis by the arm and trailed out after him.

As he was picking up bottles and glasses behind the bar, something occurred to Kominsky. There had not been a single Indian woman in the avenue that had been cleared between him and Ivan. He reared up slowly and looked at the Indians in the room, remembering some of the things he had said to Ivan. But they did not return his gaze. In groups of twos and threes, they finished the drinks they had bought before and filed silently out of the saloon.

Kominsky knew they would not be back again. In time he would forget the edge of some things, and grow to regret their absence. But now, he felt an unmistakable sense of relief when the last one of them had gone out the door.

Cornbread did not like sitting on the ground, especially on a night like this. It was frozen hard as marble, and despite his fat, the cold came through. He stole a sidelong glance at the pickup truck and thought of its warm cab and soft seats. Even the liquor seemed to be helping less the longer they sat, though the wine was better than the whiskey. It at least kept its warmth a little while longer, pushing out from his stomach into his cramped limbs. He hefted the gallon and took another pull. The wine sloshed over his lips, and some of it ran down his neck and under his shirt front like little rivulets of ice. He shivered and stretched out his legs stiffly and stood up.

Ivan did not notice him until he was standing, and then he said, "Where you going?"

"I'm gonna give Joe Ellis a drink," Cornbread mumbled.

"Leave the sonofabitch alone. He don't deserve no drink."

Cornbread hesitated. "But he ain't feelin' good," he argued.

Ivan had forgotten him. He was hunched cross-legged on the ground, the bottle of whiskey caught in the space between his crotch and his legs. Cornbread shrugged and weaved unsteadily into the sagebrush to find Joe Ellis. When he got to where he thought he was, he looked around perplexedly, stepping to one side to let the moonlight shine onto the patch of ground. Then he remembered with a chuckle to himself that this was the place Joe Ellis had been the first time they beat him up that night. He turned at right angles and went looking again.

Cornbread found him when he felt something moving under his foot. Then he realized he was standing on Joe Ellis's hand. "I'm sorry, Joe Ellis," he said. He went around the big sagebrush to the clear side and slipped down on his haunches beside the old man.

"I got a drink for you, Joe Ellis." Cornbread noticed that he was lying on his back. Remembering how cold he himself had gotten just sitting, Cornbread said to him, "You shouldn't lay like that, Joe Ellis. You ain't feelin' so good tonight."

Joe Ellis mumbled something through his smashed mouth. Cornbread leaned closer to hear. "I can't understand you. You take a drink and maybe you talk better." He put his hand behind Joe Ellis's head, lifted him up, and slopped some wine in the general direction of his face. Joe Ellis gagged and coughed, spraying the wine on Cornbread.

Cornbread pulled his hand away and let Joe Ellis drop. His head struck the ground with a little bounce. "Goddammit," Cornbread rumbled. "Don't waste the wine."

Joe Ellis had revived a little. He was whispering something. Cornbread leaned down again to catch his words. "I don't care about the pickup no more," Joe Ellis gasped. "You take it and go to Reno and leave me here."

"Okay, Joe Ellis," said Cornbread. He raised him up again and gave him another drink.

There was a frown on Cornbread's brow. He had just realized something. He stood up and went back towards the pickup, wishing that they had not wanted to go to Reno, and that they had not taken the old Fort Churchill road so that no one would see them when they beat Joe Ellis up, and that they had not beaten Joe Ellis up, and especially that they had not stopped here, with the crumbled old fort looming ghostly through the vapors that rose from the frozen ground, because the fort was doing something to Ivan. It summoned up the ghosts of white soldiers who had killed his grandfather.

Cornbread walked past Ivan to the door of the pickup and pulled it open and set the wine inside. Ivan was still sitting cross-legged on the ground. He had not moved when Cornbread walked past him.

"Ivan!" Cornbread called. When Ivan did not answer, he called, "Ja-ha-bich!" and wondered why he did and was immediately sorry for it, because tonight was not the night for Indian names. Ivan raised his head and looked at him.

Cornbread corrected himself. "Ivan, we better go home," he said thickly. "Old Joe Ellis gonna die if we don't take him home."

"You goddam right he's gonna die!"

When Cornbread finally understood what he had heard, he raised his hand. "No. No, Ivan."

"You goddam right he's gonna die!" He sprang so quickly to his feet that Cornbread stumbled backwards against the pickup in surprise. "We gonna kill him!"

Cornbread sat down suddenly on the running board of the pickup. Ivan thrust the whiskey bottle in front of his face. "You drink it!"

Cornbread looked up at him. "I rather have wine," he said, the end of it rising almost in a question.

"You leave that goddam wine alone. That's for lovin', not killin'."

Cornbread drank the whiskey, drank so much of it that the blood roared up into his head, because every time he lowered the bottle, Ivan would jam it into his mouth again. When he could take no more, Ivan raised it to his own lips and gurgled the bottle empty. He heaved it through the window of the pickup, showering glass on Cornbread's head.

"Come on, Pe-har-be," Ivan said. "We gonna kill ourselves a white man." He whooped and started a dance, but by now he was so drunk that he slipped and fell on his side. Cornbread tried to help him up, but he had no strength left, and he fell, too. They finally crawled on their hands and knees to where Joe Ellis was lying. Joe Ellis was not aware of their presence until he felt Ivan's hot breath on his face. His eyes opened a little, and then stretched wide. He started to say something, but Ivan's hands plunged onto his throat and cut it off.

Cornbread watched with growing interest. Ivan was getting nowhere. Despite his straining, Joe Ellis's eyes were still open and his nostrils were fluttering. With a sob of helplessness, Ivan rolled onto the ground and lay panting.

"He ain't dead, Ivan," Cornbread offered.

"You do it," Ivan gasped.

Cornbread shrugged and mounted Joe Ellis and tried it for a while. But he was no better off. He gritted his teeth and bore down until his arms ached, and then he gave it up and rolled onto the ground, too. He opened his eyes when he heard the sound. Ivan was astraddle Joe Ellis again, but this time he was methodically plunging his knife into his chest. Cornbread watched him detachedly. "What you doing now?" he asked.

"I'm gonna take his heart out."

But Ivan did not have the strength to part the ribs. He rested a couple of times, and then swore and gave it up. Instead, he crawled around through the brush until he found a rock and came back with it. He began beating on Joe Ellis's ankles.

"What you doing now?" Cornbread murmured again.

"Goddam, don't you know nothing?" said Ivan. "You gotta break a white man's legs so his spirit don't walk."

After a while, when the cold had cleared their heads enough so that they could stand, they went back to the pickup truck. "Now, we go to Reno and have a good time," Ivan said.

Cornbread was relieved. Ivan wasn't mad anymore. He seemed satisfied, and Cornbread knew they would have a good time in

Reno, all right. He purposely did not tell Ivan what he had seen when they left Joe Ellis. The hole in the old man's chest was still sucking air. Cornbread was too tired to bring it up.

After the pickup had roared off, crashing the frozen sagebrush every time it veered off the dirt road, Joe Ellis turned over on his stomach. He knew he was lying on the ground, but he could not remember how he had gotten there. All he knew was that he was not feeling good, and had not been all night. He raised his head and saw the wall of the old fort swimming in the vapors, and thought it was a house. He began to crawl toward it. When he reached the road he realized he could go no further, but that it didn't make any difference, because it was too late, anyway.

**T**he young lawyer looked disconsolately at the toe of his shoe and remarked vaguely to himself that he needed a shine.

"I wouldn't take it so hard," the other lawyer said. "Trial work is trial work. It'll be good experience. Do you want another drink?" He waved to the cocktail waitress without waiting for an answer.

The young lawyer, named Spencer, uncrossed his legs so that he would not have to be irritated by looking at his shoe. "Well, I wouldn't mind it so much, except that it's my first jury trial, and I got about as much chance as a snowball in hell." He did not tell the other lawyer the exact definition, that it was a hell of a way to start out a law career, sending your first client to the gas chamber. That was the kind of joke that hung on for a long time.

The other lawyer was ahead of him. "Old gasser Spence," he grinned. But when the young lawyer looked at him in quick embarrassment, he pulled off. "Maybe you can get him off with life."

The young lawyer opened his hands helplessly. "Not a chance. There were two of them in on it, and the younger one already got off with a plea because he isn't eighteen yet. I called the D.A. out there and he says the town wants blood, and my boy is it."

"How come old Judge Hoskins appointed you for it, anyway?" the other lawyer said. "Has he got something against you?"

"I don't know him hardly at all," Spencer said. "Except that we were sworn in before him. Remember he was substituting on the bench in Reno then?"

"Oh, yeah, I remember," the other lawyer said. "But it's still funny he would go sixty miles away to appoint someone. Did you say anything to rub him? He's pretty crusty. He was a saddlebag lawyer, you know, before he went up on the bench."

"I didn't say anything to him," the young lawyer said. "He said it to us. He said that for a bunch of Nevada lawyers, we sure as blazes looked like we came out of New York." The young lawyer did not mention that the judge was looking right at him when he said it, and that he had suddenly not felt quite so elegant in his Brooks Brothers suit as he had a few minutes before.

"He's always had the ovaries for the Reno lawyers," said the other lawyer defensively, who was dressed very well himself. "Maybe you can hang him up on an error. He's weak on the law, you know." He looked intense for a moment. "What are the facts? Seems to me I read a little shot about it in the papers a while back."

"I don't know," the young lawyer said. "They didn't tell me any more than I've told you. All I know is my client's name." His voice trailed off apprehensively.

The other lawyer detected it. "Well, what *is* his name?"

Spencer felt the flush creeping up on his neck. "Cornbread," he said.

"Oh, no," the other lawyer said. "You're kidding!"

As the laughter burst on his ears, the young lawyer wished he had not even brought up the case. If there were any doubt about it becoming a joke at his expense, it was removed now. Damn the breaks. It was a miserable way to start out a law career.

Old Sheriff Farrell might have been an imposing figure once, but the only thing that remained of that was his moustache. The rest of him was a study in sagging, well-contented flesh. Still, Spencer could sense that there was a hard core to him underneath.

"If you don't want me there, Mr. Lawyer," the sheriff said, "that's your right. But that ain't no white man in there. That's a Injun, and a crazy one to boot to do what he did."

"Sheriff, I want you to understand it's nothing personal," Spencer said. "But he happens to be my client and you will certainly be a witness for the prosecution. I just can't have you there."

The sheriff grinned in a manner that Spencer felt was a little condescending. "Ain't nothing he's gonna tell you that he ain't already told me."

"I know you have a confession and all that," Spencer said. "But there could be something else involved that might help his case. That's what I want to find out."

"I can tell you everything about him from the time he took his first scalp," the sheriff said. "Ain't really no reason for you to see him at all."

Spencer could not help grinning. "That's pretty funny, sheriff," he said. "Now, can I see my client?"

"That's the fanciest name he's ever been called," the sheriff said. "Almost worth doin' a killin' for, I bet that Injun will figger." He reached into a side drawer of his desk and pulled out a small pistol and laid it in front of Spencer. "If you're set on bein' in there alone with him, you better stick this in your pocket."

Spencer looked from the gun to the sheriff. The sheriff shook his head. "I ain't joshin' now," he said. "If he climbs you, I ain't takin' the responsibility."

Spencer pushed the gun away gingerly. He still was not sure whether the sheriff was giving him another taste of old frontier humor. "No, thank you, sheriff," he said. "As far as I'm concerned, that's an open invitation for trouble."

The sheriff had a little smile on his face. "You born and raised in this country, you say?"

Spencer bridled. "That's right, sheriff," he said. "Born and raised in Reno." He stood up and led the way to the back of the jail.

The cell stunk, the cot on which Spencer was sitting stunk, and Cornbread stunk worst of all. He was lying sprawled on another cot, his hands clasped behind his head, droning along in a voice that seemed to have no inflection at all.

Spencer was having a hard time taking notes. But it was not because of the smell. In stops and starts, they got through the background of it, all right. And even the argument in Kominsky's saloon only managed to give him a little thrill, as though he were beginning to sink his teeth into the meat and motives of the case. No matter if it was just another one of those "Injun things," as the sheriff said, it was still his first case. And watching Cornbread's fat hulk reclining harmlessly on the cot, Spencer had allowed himself a moment of contempt for the sheriff and his dramatic frontier business about the pistol.

And then, suddenly, the orderly process in Spencer's head came to a grinding halt, and he was not sure at all about the sheriff. He said to Cornbread, "All right. Now tell me everything about the murder that you told the sheriff in your confession, and anything else you forgot to tell him."

Spencer's mouth went dry. The cold kept washing up his back and into the base of his neck, so that he felt he could count every hair that was there. All that he had known about the case, the legal, concealing words on the complaint, ". . . did willfully and with malice aforethought murder and mutilate," ran in sterile overtone to what he was hearing. He could not look at the pock-marked face and stolid, black eyes, and he could not look away.

When it was done, he asked his first coherent question, and that only by impulse. "Why?"

Cornbread pondered a moment, looked at him in childish puzzlement, and shrugged. "I dunno."

$pencer was not a drinking man in times of stress, but since he had to go to Kominsky's saloon anyway, he had a drink. He listened inattentively to Kominsky's diatribe against all Indians and how the town felt about the killing of poor Joe Ellis, caught the fleeting question mark in the bartender's eyes in one unmasked moment, and, in turn, did his best to hide the fact that he needed the drink. Afterwards, as Cornbread had asked him to, he went to the Indian village to see Cornbread's father.

The shacks were set back and away from the town like a neglected cancer, and the outhouse smell he had smelled on Cornbread was everywhere. The paths, marked by fifty years of visiting from house to house, were packed down, and the rest of the ground was uncared-for mud. But to his mild surprise, the inside of the shack was reasonably clean. It was bare, with a wooden table and a cookstove and castoff iron beds, but reasonably clean.

He talked to the old man, who was not at all like Cornbread, but lean and white haired and with a strong old face and very old eyes that were so luminous they were almost hypnotic. Spencer learned little what would help him very much, except that the sheriff had gotten a confession out of Cornbread by threatening to tie him overnight inside the box with Joe Ellis's remains. Once, when the old man complained that it was not justice that his nephew, Ivan, who was the real troublemaker, should be allowed to live well in prison while his son had to die, the old woman who had been puttering in the background quickly went outside and gave a keening wail.

When Spencer rose to go, he remembered why he had come in the first place, and said to the old man, "Your son told me to tell you he can't sleep."

The old man nodded. "Okay. I'll fix him up."

Spencer paused uncertainly. "Do you want me to take anything to him to help him?"

The old man shook his head. "No. I'll fix him up from here." When he saw the inquiring look on Spencer's face, he said, "I'm a doctor." Spencer turned away before the slow realization he knew was in his eyes could show. Cornbread's father was a medicine man.

In the motel room, he lay on one elbow and made notes in a legal-sized tablet, and then he wrote down the names of some of the people he ought to see. As an afterthought, he jotted down the name of the district attorney. He would try to make a deal with him on a guilty plea and life imprisonment, but he already knew it was no use.

The lights of Reno were blinking on when Spencer drove down off the hills east of town. The huge, garish neons of the gambling casinos along the length of Virginia Street came on earlier than the rest of the town's lights, so that the street was like a sparkling belt through the heart of the city. The cocktail crowd at the Riverside Hotel would probably be gone home by now except for the habituals, but it didn't matter. He would find someone to have dinner with before he went home to his apartment.

Spencer found a parking place only a block away, which was luck at that. He walked through the dusk, hearing the noises of the city for the first time since he was a child. Every once in a while, a face from the courtroom would pop up in his mind and then vanish, the judge with his amused tolerance at the antics of a young lawyer in his first trial, the sheriff who was not quite so wise and sure of himself when he was on a stand under cross-examination, a sharp-faced housewife who had wanted desperately to be on the jury, but about whom Cornbread had nudged him with his elbow and said, "No good. Bad heart." That had been pretty good. Spencer would use that test again when it came to choosing a jury.

Most of the tables were empty, and Spencer sat down at one next to the wall. He would have a drink by himself and then go up to the bar and join the late stayers. He looked at the luxurious bar and its mirrors and tiers of glasses gleaming in the dim light and heard the soft, muted conversations and the high, occasional laughs. There was a quality in one of the laughing voices that reminded him of the second time he had heard the keening wail, when the jury had come back with the verdict. Then the rest of all that had happened began to come back to him. His good tiredness and satisfaction from the fact of his first trial dissolved, and he was suddenly depressed. "Christ," he said, "I might as well have been born in New York."

He waved the waitress off and went up to the bar to join the habituals, this once at least.

# THE
## GUN

From the ridge where he had paused with the sweat-streaked buckskin, he could look down upon the town below. It was a little town that lay baking in the desert sun, protected only by the occasional cottonwoods of its back streets. The yelping of a solitary dog lifted up to him from somewhere in the cluster of brown-boarded buildings.

As he watched the town, the fingers of his right hand idly found their way to the gun. They played there for a moment, almost as if they were caressing the black butt, and then moved away.

"I guess the place hasn't changed much," the rider muttered aloud, "but I never thought it was so damned little."

He leaned back in the saddle and took off the wide-brimmed hat that was thonged under his chin, so he could wipe the sweat from his forehead. He was slender but not tall, and though he carried himself loosely, there was a quickness in the way he moved his hands. His face was narrow and angular, and the thin slits of his eyes were black.

"Well, let's have a look-see at things," he said, reining the buckskin down the wagon road that led to the town. As he moved down the road, he adjusted the holster on his hip so that the black butt of the gun jutted out openly.

When he reached the outskirts, he pulled the buckskin back to a walk and moved slowly down the dusty street. Out of the corners of his eyes, he could see people turning in recognition as he rode by. In front of a saloon, a dandy with slicked hair and shined boots pushed himself away from a post and peered closely at the rider. "Tarse! Tarse Buckman!" he called excitedly. But the rider moved on without turning his head.

On the next corner, a tall man with a gray, drooping moustache stopped short with one boot raised halfway from the street to the boardwalk to watch him. The rider did not turn his head, but his lips curled in a barely perceptible sneer.

The tall man with the gray moustache raised himself to the boardwalk and stared after the rider. From a shop behind him, the butcher emerged and stood beside him on the boardwalk. "Unless my eyes are going back on me," he said, wiping his hands on his blood-spattered apron, "that was Tarse Buckman. Wasn't it, Tom?"

"It was," the tall man said. The sun glinted on the single edge of the sheriff's star that showed under his long coat. He was a man who had been strong once, but now, his wide, spare shoulders had a droop that could not be concealed. His face was creased, but his eyes still clung to a level, gray hardness.

"He grew up," the butcher said. "Wonder what he come back here for?"

The sheriff turned away. "I don't know, but I'm going to find out," he said.

The butcher watched the retreating figure for a moment. "You be careful, Tom," he called out. "He's got a gun."

"I know he's got a gun," the sheriff muttered. He quickened his long stride toward the bend in the long street, where the rider had disappeared from view.

There was a horse trough beside the saloon that was marked Dutch's. Tarse Buckman dismounted in front of it and dropped the reins. The buckskin bowed its head into the water and sucked thirstily, and Tarse took off his hat and doused his face and hair, cupping the water in his hands and holding it to his sun-darkened face.

He was standing that way, bent over the trough and blinking through his fingers, when he saw the flash of brown legs in the sun. He raised his head quickly, but the girl had already passed by. He watched her as she twisted into the doorway of the saloon.

"So our little tramp grew up into a tramp with a gun," a brittle voice said from the other side of the trough.

A dark flush leaped into Tarse's face, and he jerked around as if he had been whipped. But when he saw who had spoken, his slender frame relaxed into a slouch and he curled his lips in the loose grin that was almost a sneer. It was the sheriff, standing grimly in the dusty street.

"Well, it's Mr. Mooney," said Tarse, drying his hands on his beaded shirt front. "I was hoping the old town had changed, but I guess I hoped too much."

Tom Mooney gave no notice that he had heard the insult. "What're you doing here?" he demanded in an even voice. "Have you come back to make trouble?"

"To tell you the truth, sheriff," said Tarse, raising his eyebrows innocently, "I was just passing through. But the old town looks pretty good," he said, glancing at the saloon the girl had entered, "so I guess I'll stick around a while."

"That's what I wanted to know," the sheriff said. "If you're staying around, I'm telling you right now you're not wearing that big, fancy gun into any saloon in this town. You can sport those high-toned duds anywhere you durned please, but leave that gun on your saddle if you're going to a saloon. This is a good town, and the people in it aren't so afraid of each other anymore that they have to wear guns."

"Maybe I've been in border country, where a man has to wear a gun," said Tarse, still grinning loosely but with an ominous edge to his voice. "Maybe I've been in some pretty rough company, where a man can get killed for just looking the wrong way, much less running off at the mouth."

The sheriff ignored the veiled threat, but his face was strung taut. "No maybe about it," he said bitterly. "Your kind always finds bad company, and they always come back to hurt good people." He paused and shook his head in a gesture of disgust. "I'm glad your daddy isn't alive to see what his fighting drunkard of a son turned into."

"You know, sheriff," said Tarse. "It's a good thing you're so holy you can't pack a gun."

The sheriff whitened about the mouth. "When the time comes that I put one on," he said, his voice nearly a whisper, "you'll find out how good of a thing it is." They stared at each other across the trough in hostile silence. "Now, are you taking off that gun?"

"You don't make the laws, sheriff," said Tarse. He turned on his heel and sauntered toward the saloon.

The sheriff took one step after him, and then stopped. He was breathing heavily, and his tall frame was trembling with helpless anger. As he stood there, the dandy with the shined boots who had called out to Tarse Buckman came clumping excitedly up the boardwalk. He threw one quick, triumphant look at the sheriff and disappeared into the saloon.

The kitchen table in the little house was already set for lunch. Billy Mooney glanced at the clock again and then went to the front door to look outside.

"We might as well eat, Fran," he said to his wife. "I guess he's not coming after all." Turning back to the table, he sat down. He was young, and as tall as his father, with wide, firm shoulders and brown hair that curled stubbornly over his forehead.

"But that's not like him," said Fran. "He did say he was com-ing, didn't he?"

Billy shrugged. "I thought he did," he said. "I stopped by the jail on my way home, and he said he'd be along as soon as he paid a bill."

Fran went to the door again and opened it. She was small with blonde hair and warm, brown eyes. The print dress she wore was starched stiffly, so that it rustled when she moved. "I think I see him now," she said. "Someone just turned the corner."

"Well, that's close enough for me to start, then," said Billy, reaching for the bread. He drew his hand away hastily when Fran whirled and approached the table.

"You leave that bread alone," she said severely. "The idea, taking food before we've even sat down."

Billy leaned back in his chair and regarded her gravely. "You're a hard woman," he said.

His father's bootsteps sounded on the porch outside, but before the older man entered, Billy suddenly reached out and caught Fran by the waist. Before she could squirm away, he had kissed her. Releasing her, he cowered with his arms raised protectively above his head.

"I'm sorry, Fran," he said, grinning at the bright spots of anger in her cheeks, "but every time you get mad, something makes me kiss you. Now, if you wouldn't get mad—" He stopped when he heard his father open the kitchen door.

Tom Mooney said nothing when he came inside. He hung his hat and coat beside the door and then went to the kitchen sink to wash his hands. When he sat down, his face was sober and there was still a whiteness about his mouth.

Billy leaned forward concernedly. "What's the matter, Pop? Don't you feel good?"

Tom Mooney waited until Fran had seated herself at the table, and then he said, "Tarse Buckman's back in town."

Billy broke his bread and raised a piece to his mouth. "You shouldn't let him bother you," he said. "Maybe he's changed. He's been gone a long time, you know."

"He's changed, all right," said Tom. "He's got a gun now."

The plate in Fran's hand dropped to the table with a clatter. "I'm sorry," she said apologetically. "It slipped."

But they were not looking at her. "You mean he's packing a gun on his hip?" asked Billy, his voice flat.

"He's all heeled and dandied up like I don't know what," said Tom. He toyed with his fork for an instant. "And no one's making him take it off."

Billy's lips were colorless when he spoke. "Did he get smart with you?"

"He did, all right," said Tom, "and I went for it, losing my temper like a kid."

Fran had been sitting quietly listening to them. Now, she closed her eyes as though she had anticipated what Billy was going to say.

"You deputize me and I'll make him take that thing off," said Billy, pushing his chair away from the table.

Tom shook his head decisively. "That's just what I don't want," he said. "I want to settle this without any gunplay. It makes me sick that after all these years of people finally getting civilized in this town, one punk is going to make trouble with a gun."

"How can you say that?" demanded Billy. "You can't wait until someone gets hurt before you do anything about it."

Tom straightened and stood up. "You talk like it's my fault," he said, his voice rising. "What else can I do? The fact that people have given up wearing guns in this town is one thing. But they're not so far removed from gun days that they're going to think about putting anything on the law books about it." He moved to the door and took down his hat and coat. "I'm sorry, Fran," he said. "Guess I'm not very hungry."

Billy got up from the table and went to him. "I'm sorry, Pop," he said, placing a hand on his father's shoulder. "If you want me, I'll be down in a little while."

"All right, Billy," said Tom. "I think you better. I'm not quite sure what's right."

Billy watched as the tall figure moved slowly across the porch and down the walk to the front gate. It seemed to him that his father had become very old. The stoop in his shoulders was some-

how more pronounced than it had ever been, and there was an
uncertainty in his face that Billy could not stand to see.

Billy went back to the table and stared at his plate in silence
for a moment. Then he rose and went into the bedroom. Fran
looked at the two empty chairs and listened as the steady ticking
of the clock beat through the silence of the kitchen.

When Billy emerged from the bedroom, he was wearing a gun.
He crossed to the door before he turned to Fran. Her gaze leaped
from the gun to his unsmiling face, but she said nothing.

"If Pop comes to find me," he said, "tell him I went for a little
ride in the hills."

When he had gone, her lower lip began to tremble. But she
shook her head fiercely, and rising, she began to clear the table.
When she went to the window, it was to see Billy riding up the
street in the direction of the desert hills. She waited until the
trunk of a cottonwood cut him from view, and then she walked
swiftly into the bedroom and closed the door.

After the glaring sunlight outside, it was cool and dark in the
saloon. At the end of the bar, the girl was talking to two dusty
buckaroos in denim work clothes. They did not look around when
Tarse Buckman came in, but the girl cast a slanting glance in his
direction.

"Mexican, I'll bet," Tarse muttered to himself when he saw the
liquid blackness of her eyes. She wore a blouse fitted so loosely
that the coppery smoothness of one shoulder was exposed. Her
shining black hair was swept away from her face and clasped
severely on her neck. She glanced at Tarse again, and when she
saw him regarding her openly, she turned her back. Grinning confidently, Tarse strode to the other end of the bar.

The black hat was pulled down low over his eyes, and the barkeeper had not recognized him. He eyed Tarse's approach suspiciously, his meaty hands planted solidly on the bar. He was
a rotund man with a big stomach and red hair plastered to his
head.

Tarse leaned an elbow on the bar and tipped back his hat.
"What's the matter, Dutch? Don't you like me no more?"

The barkeeper's eyes widened in surprise. "Tarse!" he exclaimed. "I didn't know it was you. Where in blazes did you go?"

"I been around some, I'll tell you," said Tarse.

Before he could continue, the doors to the saloon burst open and the dandy with the shined boots came in. He squinted through the gloom for an instant, and then he saw Tarse and clattered across the saloon. Then he stopped up short as if in afterthought and approached him cautiously. "It's me, Duke Rowley," he said. "Don't you remember me? We used to get drunk together."

Tarse eyed him dispassionately. "I remember you," he said.

Reassured in part, Duke came closer and leaned against the bar. "You been gone a long time, Tarse," he said cheerfully. "The old town hasn't been the same without you. Seems like everybody's getting strait-laced. No one to get drunk with anymore."

Tarse turned away from him. "Let's have a drink, Dutch," he said.

Dutch shook his head. "Show me your money first," he said firmly. "I like you, Tarse, but you stuck me good last time."

"Why, I sure wouldn't have left if I'd remembered that," said Tarse innocently. "How much do I owe you?"

"Ten bucks," said the barkeeper.

Tarse turned to Duke. "Pay him," he said.

"Sure, Tarse. It's a pleasure," said Duke, reaching eagerly into his pocket. He counted out ten dollars on the bar. When he was finished, he looked at the two remaining coins in his hand and swallowed.

"What're you worrying about?" said Tarse, picking up the two coins and putting them on the bar. "That's enough for a starter."

They gulped down the raw whiskey and set their glasses on the bar. "Just like old times, Tarse," said Duke. He looked at the gun. In the half gloom of the saloon, its butt was as black as night. "That's sure some fancy gun you got," he said admiringly. "Can you shoot it pretty straight?"

"Try me and find out," said Tarse, but he was not looking at Duke. There was an expression of annoyance on his face as he stepped away from the bar to get a better view of the girl. She was laughing and joking with the two buckaroos, and her back was still turned to him.

"What's the matter, Dutch?" he said, the irritation plain in his voice. "Don't your girls talk to the special customers?"

The barkeeper was wiping a glass. "Maybe she didn't see you," he shrugged. "I'll ask her to come down here for a while."

He maneuvered his ponderous bulk down the length of the bar and leaned forward to whisper something to the girl. She shook her head and remained where she was. Behind her, the youngest of the two buckaroos inclined his head to look down the bar, where Tarse and Duke were standing expectantly.

The barkeeper shuffled back to the end of the bar. "She says she's busy. She'll be down in a little while."

Tarse slapped the flat of his hand violently down on the bar, so that the noise resounded through the saloon. "Tell her to come down now," he said loudly. "There's paying customers down here, too."

At the other end of the bar, the girl and the two buckaroos stopped talking. The barkeeper looked at Tarse, and then shrugged and began shuffling away. He stopped a few feet away from the buckaroos and gestured sternly to the girl. She moved away from the buckaroos and twisted slowly toward Tarse and Duke. Her full lips were sullen, and resentment smouldered in her black eyes.

Behind her, the youngest of the two buckaroos stepped back from the bar and stood there with his hands on his hips, looking at Tarse. The other buckaroo grasped him by the arm and pulled him back to the bar.

Duke stepped aside to let the girl pass between them. Tarse leaned against the bar and let his eyes pass lazily over her body. "What's your name?" he said.

"Joaquina," she answered grudgingly.

"What's your business?" he asked, grinning at his own joke.

Her eyes widened in anger for an instant, and then she regarded Tarse contemptuously. "Does it amuse you to insult a woman?" she asked.

Without warning, Tarse's hand shot out and caught her arm. He shook her twice, so that her hair flew loose from the clasp and tumbled about her shoulders. "Don't get smart with me," he said through his teeth. "Where I been, we know how to handle your kind."

There was a sudden clumping of boots from the other end of the bar. Tarse stepped back quickly from the girl. It was the young buckaroo.

"Keep your hands off her, you punk," the young buckaroo bit out, his eyes blazing.

The other buckaroo had followed and was standing tensely behind him. Tarse said nothing. He leaned on his elbow against the bar and regarded the young buckaroo with the easy grin that was almost a sneer. The fingers of his right hand hung near the gun, playing idly with the studded cartridge belt.

When he did not answer, the young buckaroo flushed darkly. "Come out here!" he shouted. "Let's see how tough a woman mauler is!"

Still Tarse said nothing. He stood watching the young buckaroo, but the grin on his face was beginning to fade, and his eyes had narrowed to slits. Now, the fingers of his right hand were drumming a slow, jerking tattoo on the cartridge belt. The girl and Duke had eased away from him, and he was standing alone.

When he did not answer again, the young buckaroo bent slightly as if to leap toward him. Before he could move, the other buckaroo caught him from behind and wrestled him to the front door. Shouting and squirming helplessly, the young buckaroo was propelled out of the saloon.

When they were gone, Tarse threw back his head and laughed. Duke's face was pale, and he was looking at Tarse as if he were seeing him for the first time.

"You would have killed him," the girl said accusingly.

Tarse laughed again. "You damned rights I would have killed him," he said.

The barkeeper shuffled back to them, his face sober. "They'll be back," he said. "I don't want no trouble in here."

"Maybe they will at that," said Tarse. He thought a moment and then turned to Duke. "Go get your gun," he said.

Duke backed away from him. "You're my friend, Tarse," he said. "But don't ask me to do that."

Tarse looked at him disdainfully. "Go get it," he ordered.

Duke took a deep breath. "I better have a drink first," he said.

Outside the saloon, the buckaroo whose name was Pete Foley carried his squirming brother bodily to the horse trough and heaved him in. Sputtering and shouting, he tried to climb out, but Pete pushed him down again.

"I'll drown you, Ira," he warned.

The young buckaroo finally stopped shouting. He sat in the horse trough and shook his head to get the water out of his eyes and ears. Finally he stood up and stepped out of the trough. "Thanks, Pete," he said in a subdued voice. "I don't know what got into me. I just went blind."

"He was going to shoot you," said Pete.

"I know he was," said Ira. Bending over, he picked up his hat. "Let's get it over with," he said, moving for his horse.

"What're you going to do?"

"I'm going to get a gun and kill him," said Ira.

Pete caught him by the arm. "I'm coming with you," he said, "but you got to promise me one thing?"

"I want you to come," said Ira. "What is it?"

"Give it a square shake," said Pete. "If he wants to fight it out, all right. But if he backs down, let it stay there."

The young buckaroo nodded and reached for the reins. "I promise," he said, and swung into the saddle.

They rode away together at a trot until they reached the end of the street, and then they spurred their horses into a run.

It was mid-afternoon when Tom Mooney came back to the house. Dismounting stiffly, he opened the gate and clumped up the walk. Fran was sewing quietly in her chair on the porch.

"Where's Billy?" he asked gently. He could tell that she had been crying, but he said nothing.

She did not look up, but kept on sewing. "He went for a ride," she said.

"Any particular direction?"

"In the hills," she said. Putting down her sewing, she turned to him. "He took his gun."

Tom Mooney could not meet her eyes. "I guess I should have known," he muttered. He moved to her and patted her shoulder awkwardly. "Don't worry, Fran," he said. "Everything's going to be all right." He stood beside her for a moment and then turned to go.

"Will you be home for dinner?" she called after him in a voice that was almost desperately steady.

"I don't think so," said Tom without looking back. "You better fix yourself a little bite and go to bed."

When she did not answer, he descended the steps and walked out through the gate. Mounting his horse, he reined away and then looked back at her. But the chair was empty, and she had gone inside.

Long before he reached the cottonwood hollow, he could hear the sound of Billy's shooting, echoing in deep booms across the desert ridges. Tom bowed his head and rode slowly along the cattle trail.

He pulled his horse to a stop on the lip of the hill and watched for a long time before he called out. There was a square of cardboard nailed to the trunk of a cottonwood, and Billy was shooting at it. He was standing with his long legs wide apart in the bottom of the hollow, drawing his gun and shooting. Tom reined his horse down the side.

Holstering his gun, Billy watched his father's approach. "Pretty good, huh?" he grinned, gesturing to the torn square of cardboard. "I'll make a good deputy."

Tom Mooney gazed fixedly at the cardboard. "That's the way it's got to be, huh, Billy?" he asked.

"That's the way, Pop," said Billy. "It's the only way with people like him. Once he's made trouble, you'll never take him without gunplay."

Tom tore his gaze away from the cardboard. "Let's go back and wait for it to start," he said resignedly.

Billy mounted his horse and they climbed out of the hollow. As they rode, he flipped the cylinder of the long-barreled gun and methodically loaded the chambers.

When they reached the jail, the butcher and another merchant were waiting outside. The butcher was so agitated that his feet were almost dancing on the boardwalk. He looked at the gun on Billy's hip and wagged his head. "I don't know what's got into this town today," he said, "but it seems like everybody's got a gun on."

"What're you talking about?" asked Tom.

"It looks like something's going to break loose down at Dutch's saloon," the butcher said. "First, Duke Rowley goes loping down that way with a gun strapped to his middle, and a few minutes ago them Foley boys rode down the street heeled for trouble."

Tom looked at Billy significantly. "When it starts, it really starts," he muttered. Swinging down from his horse, he walked quickly through the jail door to his desk. He had jerked open the drawer and reached inside for his gun when he heard the shooting. The sound of it came rolling like thunder down the long street. Jamming the gun into his belt, he raced for the front door.

Billy was twisting his horse nervously in a tight circle. "Come on, Pop," he shouted. "It's started."

**D**uke Rowley poked his head out of the doorway to the saloon and looked down the length of the street. There was no sign of the two buckaroos.

"I don't see 'em," he said, stepping back inside. "Maybe they're not coming," he said hopefully, and began to walk toward the bar.

Tarse was getting drunk. His hat was tipped back on his head and there were hot flushes about his eyes. "Get back there," he yelled raucously at Duke. "You want to get me killed?"

"I could sure use a drink," said Duke, working his tongue through dry lips.

"Take him one," ordered Tarse, handing the bottle to the girl. She took it without looking up. There were deep finger marks on her bare shoulder.

Duke raised the bottle and took a swallow. His face was pale, and on his thin hips, the gun looked big and unwieldy. Lowering the bottle, he turned to Tarse again and essayed a grin. "If they don't come pretty soon," he said. "I think maybe I better go. I got to meet my girl tonight."

"Get back there," yelled Tarse, and Duke retreated to the door.

He stood there uncertainly for a moment and then straightened as running hoofbeats sounded in the street. Hesitantly, he peeked out and then pulled his head back in.

"They're coming," he said hoarsely.

At his words, Tarse spun around, spilling the bottle as he did. It rolled down the bar, whiskey sloshing out of its mouth, and fell to the floor with a crash.

Behind the bar, Dutch intoned hopelessly, "I don't want no trouble in here." But no one was listening. Outside, the hoofbeats stopped and the street was silent.

Duke had backed away from the door and was standing with his arms dangling limply at his sides. Tarse pushed him roughly. "Take the one on the left," he ordered in a harsh whisper. There was a clumping of boots on the boardwalk.

Tarse's fingers closed over the black butt of the gun. Easing it from the holster, he cocked the hammer and held it in front of him, aimed at the doorway.

Duke's eyes widened in disbelief when he saw the gun already in Tarse's hand. From the bar, Dutch croaked, "My God, give them a chance."

They came through the doors together, the young buckaroo on the right and his brother on the left. Ira Foley never knew what happened. The slugs crashed into his chest and lifted him backwards into the doorway. There was a look of horror on his brother's face. His legs buckled under him, and he dropped to his knees, his hands in front of him with palms outstretched, as though to stop the bullets. The black gun in Tarse's hand boomed out twice more. The buckaroo's head dropped between his knees and he pitched sideways to the floor.

No one spoke. The blue smoke hung heavy and acrid in the saloon as they stood without moving and stared at the bodies of the buckaroos. Duke was shaking violently. His gun was still in its holster. Down the bar, Dutch placed one of his big hands on the girl's and clasped it tightly.

"Damn fine help you are," Tarse bit out at Duke. "You could a got me killed."

Duke turned, his hands raised imploringly. But before he could say anything, they heard again the sound of running horses. Tarse jerked around to listen. Then he pushed Duke toward the doorway. "See who the hell's coming," he ordered sharply.

Duke moved weakly to the doorway and looked out. "It's the sheriff," he said hoarsely.

Tarse holstered his gun quickly. He looked around the saloon. "It was self-defense," he shrilled commandingly. "I was protecting myself."

Duke was almost tottering as he moved away from the door. Tarse grabbed him by the arm and threw him against the bar. "You tell 'em that," he rasped. "You hear? You tell 'em I was protecting myself!"

Tom Mooney was the first to come in the door. His gun was still in his belt. He looked down at the two bodies and then at Tarse and Duke, standing stock-still near the bar. Billy moved inside and stood beside his father. He did not look down, but stared steadily at Tarse, his face taut and expectant and his hand on the butt of his gun.

Before they could speak, Tarse said in a tight voice, "It was self-defense. I was—"

Down the bar, the girl suddenly ran for the back door. "It was murder!" she screamed as she ran.

Tarse's face went livid. He turned as if to pursue her, and then he whirled back. His hand moved like a snake for the black butt. The gun seemed to roar even as his fingers found it. Billy Mooney felt the wind of the bullet as he threw himself sideways.

But on the heels of the first shot, there was another shot, so closely behind that the crashing echoes seemed to blend. It was as though Tarse had been cut down with an axe. He plummeted to the floor and lay there on his face, his back broken.

They stared at Duke Rowley and the wisp of smoke that was

curling away from the muzzle of the gun in his hands. After a moment, Billy went to him and quietly took the gun from his trembling fingers. Duke did not seem to notice it was gone. He was looking down at the body of Tarse, lying at his feet.

Tom Mooney joined Billy, and together, they helped Duke to a chair at the side of the saloon. He collapsed into it.

"It's all right, Duke," said Billy, gripping him by the shoulder.

Duke looked up at them, his face wet with sweat and his eyes beseeching. "Maybe I did wrong," he said, "but I don't think so. All of a sudden, I was afraid to death of him and his gun. I was so sick I had to do something."

Tom Mooney turned away from him and looked at the body of Tarse Buckman where it lay on the floor. He knew with a quiet certainty that the time of the gun was gone forever from his town. He looked at the hand, still curled around the black butt. But now the fingers were dead, and the gun did not seem menacing at all.

# THE
# LAW
# COMES
# TO
# VIRGINIA
# CITY

Above the bar of the St. Nicholas saloon, there hung a picture of General U. S. Grant at the mouth of a Virginia City mine shaft. He was garbed in oilskins and a slouch hat, and he was standing in comradely fashion next to a muscled miner who was stripped to the waist.

Both smiled down on the high old bar of the St. Nicholas, with its little displays of gold nuggets, postcards, and tourist knick-knacks, and a group of schoolchildren indulging in a noonday bottle of soda pop. But the miner, whose head was averted slightly, seemed to be smiling in particular on the head of Cletus Cobb, relaxing on his visiting stool behind the bar.

Cletus Cobb was complacent with the air of one who has served his community well. Agatha Winston, the poetess, had just brought him the news that Tom Peel had that morning been sworn in as Virginia City's new sheriff. Cletus Cobb listened idly to the chatter of the schoolchildren, nodded once in a while to Agatha Winston's poetic ramblings, and meditated on the fact that he was responsible for Tom Peel's election. He lifted his gaze to the miner on the wall, as if acknowledging the blessing of grandfather Tyrus Cobb.

So benign was he that he remained unperturbed even when Joe Martin, the crusty little buckaroo from down the canyon, ambled into the St. Nicholas. Joe Martin made the long horseback trip to Virginia City only twice a year, and when he did, it was for a specific purpose. He had a leathery face lined with a thousand creases, and a drooping moustache that was gray and stained with tobacco. Folks said he was so ancient he could remember gun-fighting days on C street.

"Get that cat-lickin' look offen your face, Cletus Cobb," he scowled in greeting.

"I got reason to be tickled, old-timer," said Cletus placidly.

Joe Martin sniffed and darted his sharp little eyes in disapproval at the noisy schoolchildren. When he noticed Agatha Winston sitting aloofly on a stool, he touched his hand to his big hat. "Don't believe I've had the pleasure," he said.

"Oh, yes you have!" flared Agatha, tossing her head. She had straight brown hair drawn severely and artistically back. "I'm not forgetting what you said to me the last time you were in town."

Joe Martin regarded her impassively, and then turned to Cletus. "What're you so gin-kickin happy about?"

"We got ourselves a new sheriff today," said Cletus.

"What the hell was wrong with Gentle Eddie?" asked Joe Martin.

Cletus shook his head regretfully. "He just didn't prove up. Couple months back, someone tried to hold up Pat Malley at the Old Leaning Rail. Pat ran him out with the General Grant saber, and then he called Eddie to come down and arrest the man. But Eddie just went back to bed."

"Always knew that boy had some sense," said Joe Martin. "Can't say the same for some people I know."

Cletus ignored the jibe. "This new man looks pretty good to me," he said. "Quiet sort, but you can tell he's got iron underneath."

"Why the hell anybody would wanna be sheriff—" muttered Joe Martin.

"It's basic," offered Agatha, who had given up her job to come to Virginia City and be a poetess. "Every man must find his function in life. Without work, civilization would have no purpose, and man would be cast adrift on a sea of no ports."

When Joe Martin swore at her, Agatha leaped from the stool. "He said it again!" she cried.

Before Cletus could intervene, Joe Martin turned and stamped away. "Why in the hell it's so durned tough to get a drink in this town anymore—" he shot back at Cletus and slammed out through the doors.

It was some time before Agatha could compose herself. When she did, she bade Cletus a pained good afternoon and went out. She was back so fast that Cletus blinked.

"Take a look for yourself!" she fluttered.

"Take a look at what?" asked Cletus without getting off his stool.

Before she could answer, the doors opened and a figure was framed in the doorway. Cletus Cobb leaned forward on his stool and squinted in disbelief. Though the bright sunlight glaring in from the street outside made it hard to see, he could have sworn there were the outlines of two guns jutting from the hips of the figure in the doorway.

"You kids get out of this saloon!"

Recognizing Tom Peel's voice, Cletus chuckled and relaxed again on his stool. So the new sheriff had a sense of humor. Well, that spoke well of any man.

Tom Peel strode with measured tread to the middle of the saloon. "I'm not telling you again," he said to the row of open mouths and round eyes at the bar. "When I say get, that means get!"

The little people looked uncertainly from the sheriff to Cletus

Cobb, and one of them warily set his bottle on the bar and reached up to recover his books. Cletus Cobb stood up. By gosh, there *were* two guns, nestled in open holsters that were tied down. More than that, Tom Peel's black handlebar moustache had suddenly acquired meaning. Above it, there was a black sombrero, and beneath it, there was a black vest on which the sheriff's star glinted ominously.

"Holy jumping Jenny!" exclaimed Cletus. Though he was coming to expect a lot of things in Virginia City of late, it was still too early in the day for this. "What's happened to you, Peel?" he said, remembering the lean-faced but amiable candidate he had personally squired about town for more than a month.

"I'll thank you to call me sheriff," said Tom Peel icily.

Cletus Cobb was nettled, but he regarded the sheriff's star on Peel's black vest and held himself in check. "All right, then, sheriff it is," he said. "Though sheriff it wouldn't be this day if it wasn't for me."

"I'm obliged to you," said Tom Peel. "But that doesn't happen to be what I came in here about."

Cletus was losing control of himself. "Now, hold on there," he said. "I want to get this straight. Do you mean to tell me you're running these kids out of my saloon?"

"I believe there's a law to that effect."

"The law go to blazes!" bellowed Cletus. "Young'uns in Virginia City always drink their soda pop in the saloons. Did it myself when I was a kid."

"That's nice," said Tom Peel. He turned to the hushed group huddled in front of the bar. "Now, get out of here!"

Cletus Cobb was a big man with sloping muscles. He moved out indignantly from behind the bar. "You asked for this," he said in a tight voice.

Tom Peel held his ground. He made no move except to drop his hand quickly to the general vicinity of a gun butt. It hung there, fingers poised to drop, as Cletus Cobb drew up short with his mouth ajar in shocked surprise.

"Make your play, Cobb," said the sheriff.

Cletus Cobb was still standing in the same place when Sheriff

Tom Peel herded the youngsters out into the street and sent them on to school. When Cletus could finally speak, he said hoarsely, "Why, that goddam fool was going to shoot me."

Grandfather Tyrus Cobb had been among the first of the Cornishmen to come from England to work in the deep mines of the Comstock, and Cletus was thereby of the royal blood of Virginia City. The oldest of the families on the hill and the latest of the retreating artists looked to him for guidance.

Even now, Agatha Winston was watching him in mute supplication. When she saw that nothing constructive was forthcoming, she said airily, "It's such a nice day I think I'll go for a walk down the street."

"Oh sure, spread the word," said Cletus angrily. But Agatha only tossed her head and took leave.

Cletus Cobb was outraged, not only at the way he had been taken in by a stranger, but because he had disregarded a twinge of misgiving the day Tom Peel said he wanted to be sheriff. Before that, Cletus had regarded the black moustache without emotion, but on that day it had seemed to hint of something.

He had even listened in Pat Malley's Old Leaning Rail saloon when Bob Winters, the artist, had sounded the same doubt by saying it reminded him of something he couldn't quite put his finger on. But Pat Malley, who was at odds with Gentle Eddie, had reminded both of them that a number of the good people of Virginia City still wore moustaches, and at least Tom Peel didn't wear long hair and a goatee like Buffalo Bill Hestler.

It was then that Cletus Cobb pushed away his unfounded doubts and nobly admitted Pat Malley was right. And when the skeptical Winters had said he didn't like the ring of Tom Peel's campaign slogan—"Law and Order in Virginia City"—Cletus Cobb scoffed him down.

Upon remembering this incident, however, Cletus Cobb strangely felt a little better. At least, he was not alone in the blame. If the truth be known, it was Pat Malley who had done the convincing about Tom Peel. Cletus Cobb dwelled on this at length, and finally took off his apron, closed the door of the St. Nicholas, and stalked righteously in the direction of the Old Leaning Rail to take the matter up with Pat Malley.

He had moved only a block when he saw Sheriff Tom Peel standing on the boardwalk with his back to him. Cletus was about to cross the street in a gesture of contempt when he saw something else. Buffalo Bill Hestler was walking down the boardwalk toward the sheriff. There was something portentous about the situation, and Cletus ducked into the Washoe Corner saloon to watch.

As was his custom, Buffalo Bill Hestler was on his way to the Washoe Corner to collect an afternoon drink. During the tourist season, he was a landmark of sorts in Virginia City, with his long hair and goatee and a costume that included high boots and pearl-handled guns. He worked long hours in the summers, moving from one saloon to another, for which adornment he collected enough retainers and drinking privileges from the proprietors to last him through the winter months. He was probably the most photographed shill in the nation.

He was also a little nearsighted, so that he did not seem to comprehend the significance of the tall and square-shouldered figure blocking the boardwalk. He almost collided with Sheriff Tom Peel before he was aware of his presence.

"Well, it's Tom," he exclaimed, squinting from under his eyebrows at the sheriff. "I been meaning to shake your hand by way of congratulations." He put out his hand.

Sheriff Tom Peel ignored the gesture. "What're you doing with those guns on?" he said sternly.

Buffalo Bill had never been confronted with such a question. His guns were as much a part of him as his goatee. He deliberated it for a moment, and then grinned self-consciously, as though he had concluded Tom Peel was kidding him. But upon closer scrutiny, he could find no trace of humor in the sheriff's face. Buffalo Bill was at a loss for an answer.

"I don't know, sheriff," he said plaintively.

"Well, get 'em off and keep 'em off," said Tom Peel. "There'll be no more gun packing on this street as long as I'm sheriff."

"But they're empty," Buffalo Bill protested. "As far as I know, they ain't never been shot." And he reached for one to prove his point.

From the protection of the Washoe Corner saloon, Cletus Cobb had to admit the sheriff was handy. Hardly had Buffalo Bill Hestler's hand dropped to the butt of his pistol than he was staring into the black muzzle of Tom Peel's .45.

Buffalo Bill had never viewed a gun from this position. It confused him no end. He staggered back with his elbow drawn up in front of him as though to ward off a bullet. "I give up, sheriff!" he called out in panic.

The answer seemed to suit Tom Peel. He took two long steps toward Buffalo Bill and jerked loose the buckle of his gunbelt. Holstering his own gun, he turned away. "You can pick these up in a box," he said.

Buffalo Bill watched him go. He was still leaning shakenly against a wooden railing when Cletus Cobb emerged from the Washoe Corner saloon. "Afternoon, Bill," Cletus murmured, and considerately averted his head.

With a covert glance at the sheriff's retreating figure, Cletus crossed the street toward the Old Leaning Rail. He jumped to the boardwalk so savagely that Joe Martin's dozing mustang snorted and shied away.

Cletus pushed open the door. "Are you happy now, Pat Malley?" he demanded.

Pat Malley, who was short and broad and florid-faced, was by this time completely out of sorts with the world. On one hand, he had witnessed the scene between the sheriff and Buffalo Bill, and it was weighing heavily upon him. On the other, Joe Martin was drinking at the end of the bar, and he had already begun to throw things.

"I knew you were over there thinking that," he cried. "Now, you're going to put the whole thing on me."

"It was you who said there was nothing wrong with his moustache," Cletus challenged.

Pat Malley blinked. "What the devil has that got to do with it?" he said.

Bob Winters, the artist, skittered hastily into the saloon. He was dressed as usual in sweatshirt and denims. "What did I tell you?" he said triumphantly.

"What *did* you tell us?" asked Pat Malley with polite scorn.

"It all fits now," said Winters. "That character thinks he's back in the Old West. I knew there was something behind that handlebar moustache and that Law and Order pitch."

"Don't you try to beg out of this one," cried Cletus.

Bob Winters raised his hands helplessly. "I wasn't trying—" he began.

There was a shattering crackle of glass from the far end of the bar. "Tyrus Cobb and Timothy Malley, will you shuddup for the sake of Nell!" It was Joe Martin. There was already a growing pile of broken beer and whiskey bottles surrounding the cast-iron stove in the corner of the saloon, and the old buckaroo had just added another to emphasize his demand.

"Now dammit, Martin, watch your aim!" shouted Pat Malley, observing irritably that the last bottle had broken considerably to the left of the stove. But Joe Martin didn't hear him; after his outburst, he had resumed his solitary grumbling.

"The night yet to come and he's already back to grandfather Timothy's time," moaned Pat Malley. "What'll it be like by morning?" Then, as if in sudden thought, he wheeled on Cletus Cobb. "He came into your place first. It was your turn this time."

Before Cletus could answer, Agatha Winston flitted in the door with the air of someone who has found her playmates in trouble. "You people have been making too much noise in here," she said accusingly. "And guess who's coming to make you stop?"

The tumult in the Old Leaning Rail saloon came to a sudden stop, and the occupants were staring quietly at the door when the sheriff came in. In the gloom of the late afternoon, he was a lean and threatening figure in his black moustache and with the light slanting dull off his star and gun butts.

"What's going on in here?" he demanded in a hard voice.

No one offered to enlighten him, and there was a long and pregnant silence. "Speak up," he said commandingly.

In the stillness, the shattering of the glass was deafening. The sheriff started, then stepped clear of the group so that he could see the end of the bar. Cletus Cobb closed his eyes, but Joe Martin, heedless of what was going on, was in the process of emptying another bottle of beer into his chaser glass.

The sheriff took a closer look and saw that the back corner of the saloon was littered with broken bottles. "What's he doing?" he said with the least hint of incredulity in his voice.

"Breaking bottles," said Agatha Winston helpfully.

The sheriff's baffled gaze leaped from one face to another, but there was no help there. No one seemed to think anything unusual was happening. And while the sheriff was thus occupied, there was another splintering crash.

The sheriff jerked again. His voice was beginning to show some emotion. "Make him cut that out," he told Pat Malley. "It's your place of business."

"I don't mind," said Pat Malley.

"Make him cut that out," the Sheriff repeated. "He's disturbing the peace."

Pat Malley sighed and moved slowly down to the end of the bar. There was wariness in his approach. He leaned forward to Joe Martin.

"Martin," he said, "the sheriff wants you to cut that out."

After a moment, Joe Martin recognized Pat's presence. He tipped his big hat back on his head and pushed his face over the bar.

"What's your trouble, Timothy Malley?"

"Pat," corrected Pat Malley. "Cut out throwing the bottles," he said. "The sheriff doesn't want you to throw any more bottles."

"Whatta you mean by sheriff?" asked Joe Martin. "I thought we buried him last week."

Pat Malley inclined his head toward the front of the saloon, and Joe Martin's head slowly followed. His sharp little eyes picked out the sheriff, and he straightened on his stool with a snap. "Well, I'll be durned," he said. "It's Wild Bill Hickok!"

Agatha Winston giggled and Cletus Cobb blanched. There was a rush of color to Sheriff Tom Peel's face. He seemed to be at a loss for anything new to say. "Cut that out," he said.

Joe Martin regarded him for a moment, and then turned away

and solemnly emptied the beer bottle into his glass. When he was done, he took hold of the bottle by the neck and turned around to throw it at the sheriff.

"For God's sake, no!" choked Cletus Cobb as Joe Martin raised the bottle.

Cletus had been watching Joe Martin, so that the first inkling of what had happened came when the bottle disintegrated in the old buckaroo's hand and the mirror in back of the bar suddenly acquired a cobweb pattern. It was a few seconds before Cletus realized that the ringing in his ears had been caused by the sheriff's .45. He was standing in a haze of blue smoke.

"Goddammit, look at my mirror!" said Pat Malley.

It was a legitimate request, Cletus conceded. The old mirror was something to look at. By some miracle, it had held intact, but the complete face of it was lined with spidery breaks radiating away from a round hole near the base.

Joe Martin had not moved. He was sitting on his stool, looking first at the broken neck of the bottle in his hand, and then at the sheriff.

After a moment, he slid down off the stool and rocked unsteadily on his bowed little legs toward the door. Cletus stepped aside to let him pass, but Joe Martin paused before he went out to say something to the sheriff.

"Don't leave town, mister," he said ominously. "I'll be back by morning." He edged out the door; they heard his clumping on the boardwalk and, in a moment, the retreating hoofbeats of his horse.

The sheriff had holstered his gun. He seemed to have recovered his composure. "What did he mean by that?" he said harshly.

Cletus Cobb turned to face the sheriff. "He means he's going after his gun," he said in an accusing tone.

"That's his business," said the sheriff. "It's not my concern until he comes after me."

Cletus's eyes widened. "You're not going to gunfight him!"

"It's my duty," said Tom Peel. "I wouldn't be worth my salt as a sheriff if I backed down to a gunslinger."

Cletus regarded him helplessly, and then changed his tack.

"In case you haven't heard, sheriff," he said, "Joe Martin was a real gunfighter in his day." Cletus was not quite sure whether he should let himself be carried away like this, but he could not stop now. "I can still remember my grandpa telling me about the time Joe Martin blew the heads off three freshcomers, right in that street out there."

Sheriff Tom Peel's expression did not change. "I'll be waiting for him," he said in a low voice. His shoulders were squared when he went out the door.

"One hundred years that mirror's been there," said Pat Malley.

Agatha Winston contemplated the mirror. "It's sad in a way," she sighed. "Think of all the faces and memories it's held."

Bob Winters had moved over so that he was looking directly into the cobweb of tiny breaks. "Not bad at that," he mused aloud, moving his head back and forth. "It gives you sort of an unhinged feeling, like a jigsaw puzzle. I wonder how a self-portrait on the abstract side would work out."

"You could call it Reflections of Sunday Morn at the Old Leaning Rail," Agatha Winston suggested.

"Too long," said Bob Winters, "but it has possibilities."

"You think you're pretty damned funny, don't you?" said Pat Malley. The flush was rising over his white collar again.

"But I'm serious—" began Bob Winters.

Cletus Cobb pounded his big fist on the bar. "Now, cut that stuff out," he said.

"That sounds familiar," said Agatha Winston.

"I'm not joking," said Cletus Cobb angrily. "There's going to be trouble in that street out there come morning, and we have to stop it."

Bob Winters shook his head. "No such luck, Clete," he said. "Joe Martin will be all sobered up and right back in the present by the time he reaches the ranch. He won't even remember what he went home for."

"I don't know," said Cletus uncertainly. "I don't trust that old coot."

Bob Winters shrugged. "Well, I don't see where we've got much to lose anyway—a lunatic sheriff on one hand, or—"

Cletus Cobb was incensed. "That's one hell of an attitude to take."

Bob Winters raised his hands. "I was only joking."

"Well, cut that stuff out," began Cletus, and stopped. This time, even Pat Malley had a smirk on his face. Cletus pounded the bar in a thunderous effort to recover the situation.

**S**hafts of beginning light were probing their way into deserted C Street when Joe Martin came back to Virginia City. His arrival was announced by a measured and solitary clip-clop that echoed among the weathered wooden buildings and the boardwalks.

Cletus Cobb had been sulking. Everyone had made much of his anxiety, and yet at the same time, not one of them had gone home. Now, when the sound of hoofbeats came to them, they rushed to the windows as if they had been expecting it all along.

Not only had Joe Martin returned, but as far as Cletus could see, he was sober. The big sombrero was set straight on his head, and the tips of his handlebar moustache rose and fell with the motion of the horse. More significantly, his right hand was hanging free by his side.

"What did I say?" demanded Cletus. "He's got a gun."

"Good God, look at the size of that thing," said Bob Winters. "It's as long as his leg."

Joe Martin reined his horse past the jail in a bridled trot. The only indication he gave that he was conscious of its presence was a slight edging of his head in that direction until it was behind him. When he passed the Old Leaning Rail, he glanced toward the light that filtered from the high windows, and then bent his head and rode on.

He rode the full length of C Street, past the business houses, to an abandoned livery stable at the end of the boardwalk. Both horse and rider disappeared inside, and C Street was again deserted.

When Tom Peel appeared in the doorway of the jail, his face was white and drawn. The moustache had never looked blacker. From the rigidity of his movements as he descended the stoop and stood in the street, Cletus could see that he was at a fine point of tension.

Agatha Winston drew back momentarily from the window. "I

hope they can both shoot well," she said. "This window isn't very thick."

Cletus Cobb swore silently. As he watched, Joe Martin emerged from the livery stable, moved slowly to the middle of the street, and turned so that he was facing down it. Though he seemed sober, or pretty nearly so, his shoulders were more stooped than Cletus Cobb had ever seen them.

The little buckaroo stood alone in the street, and his eyes coursed the length of the boardwalk, seeking out the sheriff. But either the jail was too far away or Tom Peel was out of his line of vision, because Joe Martin did not appear to see him. He cocked his head as if listening for footsteps.

It came to him then, the crisp sound of crunching boots. Joe Martin straightened whiplike when the lean figure of Tom Peel came into view. The sheriff was making his own move to the middle of the street. And as he did, he half lifted his right-hand gun out of the holster to loosen its hold.

It was only then that realization came home to Bob Winters. "By God," he exclaimed. "Someone's going to get killed out there!"

Cletus Cobb bit savagely down on his underlip and started toward the door. Pat Malley reached out a hand. "If you're going out there to stop this," said Pat, "then shake my hand now. You won't be around to do it again."

Cletus Cobb looked at Pat Malley for a long moment, and then returned to his place at the window.

When the sheriff reached the middle of the street, he turned exactly as Joe Martin had done. They stood facing each other, nearly a full block apart. It was Joe Martin's turn to move, and he did, faltering almost imperceptibly and then taking a step forward. At the other end of the street, Sheriff Tom Peel began his walk. The gap between them began to close.

"Was that true what you said about Joe Martin shooting heads off?" wailed Agatha Winston. But Cletus could not answer. His throat had constricted.

And then Joe Martin stopped. He had been moving forward in the only ambling gait that his bent legs would permit. But slowly, before it was time, it dwindled and came to a halt. He looked about him and then shook his head as if trying to break something loose from his mind. He glanced at the lighted windows of the Old Leaning Rail, and then at the sheriff. He stood without moving, with the morning light full on his creased face, as though seeing the sheriff for the first time.

Tom Peel had been in full stride when Joe Martin stopped. The action surprised him, since it was not yet time, and he jarred to a rude halt. A flicker of irritation crossed his face.

When Joe Martin began to walk again, Cletus Cobb drew in his breath sharply. But the tightness was gone from the old buckaroo's movements. As he ambled forward, he was not looking at the sheriff anymore. His eyes were fixed on the ground.

When the advance resumed, Tom Peel took a decisive step forward. His face was set expectantly, and he began to crouch a little. But when he saw that Joe Martin was not even looking at him, he straightened in his tracks and stopped, perplexity and anger in his face.

Joe Martin did not stop. He moved steadily toward Tom Peel, his head still bowed. He was past the interval when he should have come to the last halt, but he moved slowly forward into point blank range.

Tom Peel's hand went down to his gun and stayed there, fingers wrapped about the butt. "Draw, damn you! Draw!" he shouted.

But Joe Martin did not draw. When he was face to face with the sheriff, he looked up for the first time. They stared at each other in silence. Tom Peel was shaking in frustration. Joe Martin reached up a leathery hand and clapped it in gentle understanding on his shoulder.

"It's no good, boy," he said. "We can't bring it back. It's too late."

Tom Peel stared white-faced at Joe Martin. He began to tremble violently. When it passed, he closed his eyes as though in weariness.

"Come on, boy," said Joe Martin. "I'll buy you a drink."

Tom Peel's chest rose and fell with a long sigh. He shook his head. "Some other time, old-timer," he said. He turned from Joe Martin and walked away.

Joe Martin watched him for a moment, and then started in the direction of the Old Leaning Rail. There was noticeably more purpose in his walk.

Later in the day, Cletus Cobb dropped into the Old Leaning Rail for an afternoon drink. Things seemed to be riding at normal, he observed. Joe Martin was drinking at the end of the bar, and the pile of broken bottles in the corner was becoming formidable. Bob Winters had been serious, after all. With Agatha Winston hovering near, he was painting a self-portrait from his reflection in Pat Malley's broken mirror.

"Don't know if you heard, Pat," said Cletus with a general air of satisfaction. "But Tom Peel shaved off his moustache."

"I heard," said Pat Malley.

"Guess you're the only one who got hurt after all," said Cletus, nodding toward the mirror.

"Oh, I wouldn't say that," said Pat Malley with a sly smile. "I plan to do a right good business on account of that mirror. He put his elbows down on the bar and leaned toward Cletus Cobb. "Yessir, mister," he said seriously. "That's an authentic bullet hole. Happened in my grandpa's time. Seems there was this gunslinger come to town one day . . ."

# THE

## HERD

## STALKER

The dog stood motionless on the grassy knoll, his hackles raised and his shoulders hulked forward.

Overhead, the moon hung poised in the sky for a long moment, and then scudded into the inky blackness of a cloud. A sombre gloom settled over the high plateau. The pines ceased their hushed whispering and stood silent.

Below the knoll, in the soft sand that was the bed ground, the sheep had wakened from their sleep. Singly and in groups, they rose and faced as one to the side where the plateau sloped into the midnight cavern of the forest. The lambs slept on.

On the high knoll, the dog hesitated, his forelegs quivering.

Then he turned and trotted stiff-legged down the slope to the darkened camp. At the entrance to the tent, he stopped and looked back toward the bed ground.

Reluctantly, the dog turned and skirted the cold fire pit and trotted back to the high place on the knoll. As he lifted his nose to the night breeze, his hackles bristled again, and a growl was born in his chest.

But the growl died in a whimper, and the dog again turned away from the knoll and slunk back slowly to the camp.

Beneath the open flap of the tent, he paused and then entered into the darkness. As he passed the canvas bed on the pine boughs, a shaggy haunch brushed the sleeping face of Jean Baptiste.

The herder sniffed and sputtered to drowsy wakefulness. A head crested with an awry mass of hair appeared above the blankets.

"*Ekhen hadi hortic!* Get out of here, dog!" The command croaked out through lips thickened with sleep. It carried with it a tone of expected obedience, but the dog only whimpered from the far dark corner of the tent.

The herder raised himself in the bed and blinked in disbelief. But the curse on his lips was stilled by the sudden rumble of hooves and the lone, agonized bleat from the night outside. The meaning of the sounds coursed through the herder like an electric current.

"*Mon Dieu,* the *liona!*" he gasped out in a mixture of French and Basque as he fought to disentangle himself from the blankets. Leaping from the bed, he jerked on his boots and Levi's, groped blindly for the carbine and lantern, and burst out of the tent at a dead run.

He hauled up short when he saw the sheep bowling down from the bed ground in a direct path toward the camp. Bracing his legs, he fought to keep his balance in the sea of jolting forms that swept past him.

Then, when the wave had passed, the herder pounded up the slope and onto the sand flat, levering a cartridge into the chamber of the carbine as he ran. A sideward glance showed him the ewes who had been too frightened to run, and he plowed through the sand in the direction toward which they faced, to the side where the bed ground planed off into the pines.

Above him, the moon sidled slowly from behind the cloud, and the plateau was bathed again with its pale light. The herder came to a halt at the crest of the ridge, where the deep shadows began, and listened. But the night was silent. There was only the sound of his own heavy breathing in his ears. The sheep had stopped their stampede. The mountain lion was gone.

The herder knelt in the sand and fumbled for a match. Cupping the flickering flame in one broad hand, he touched it to the wick of the kerosene lantern. His face, grim and hard, was outlined in the soft flare of light.

With the lantern raised high in the air, the herder searched through the manzanita clumps and the trees for that which he knew he would find.

The light caught and held on a mottled pool of brilliance below a small boulder covered with manzanita. The herder held the lantern forward and myriad leaves, all speckled with the same brilliance, winked back at him. And there, behind the boulder and the manzanita, where they had lain to sleep, were the lambs.

The herder stood above them, playing the lantern on the mutilated forms. The heads of two were twisted back, at odds with the line of their bodies, and their throats were bloody and ravaged. The head of the third lamb had been ripped away. Its underside was a dark gouge from which the stomach had been torn.

"*Gaychuak.* Poor things," the herder muttered, his voice tight with emotion. And suddenly, he was filled with a terrible rage at the thing that was happening to his herd. He raised a clenched fist toward the darkness of the forest.

"*Debria liona.* Devil lion," he choked out, "the time will come . . ." The words trailed off and the herder's shoulders slumped helplessly. He heaved a sigh, and then knelt to strip the pelts away from the lambs.

Dawn had faded away the stars in the skies to the east when he finished. The great pines were taking shape in the cold, gray light, and the Sierra was locked in stillness as the things of the forest

THE HERD STALKER 75

awaited the birth of the new day. A coyote yipped in the far distance, and the spell was broken. The herder rose to his feet and walked back across the bed ground. A ewe called as he passed with the pelt of her lamb.

The herder laid the pelts carefully across the tent rope, the wet linings toward the rising sun. Then he turned and stared down the canyons from which Laxague would come. It was the fifth day, the day for supplies, and Laxague would be at the plateau by midday, he remembered. The thought of what he would have to tell the man twisted Jean Baptiste's lips into a bitter grimace. Shaking his head ruefully, he bent to scoop up a handful of pine needles for the fire.

The two men sat cross-legged beside the small, worn square of canvas on which the noon meal was spread. The sun was high overhead, and near the plateau the sheep dozed beneath the shade of the pines. Behind the camp, the two horses of Laxague blinked sleepily and swished their tails at the buzzing flies.

Jean Baptiste looked up from his plate and saw Laxague's eyes travel again to the pelts, and the hard lines of anger return to his leathery face. Jean Baptiste reached for the dutch oven quickly.

"More *omeletta*, Laxague?" he asked.

Laxague ignored the offering. "You did not see him at all?" he asked, and the question was tinged faintly with accusation.

Jean Baptiste returned the dutch oven to the curved iron that bridged the fire pit. "No, he was gone when I reached the slope."

"What of Barbo?" Laxague persisted. "Did he not bark?"

The dog's ears pricked up at the mention of his name, and he wagged his tail furiously. Jean Baptiste caught the shaggy head in one hand and fondled it roughly.

"Yes, but it was too late," he lied. He knew that Laxague would not understand, that Barbo was afraid, that the memory of his only meeting with the lion was burned as deeply as the wound that had lain his shoulder open to the bone. The dog had been saved only by the sound of the herder's approach. Jean Baptiste had found Barbo where the lion had turned on him, in the clearing below the quaking aspen.

Laxague's eyes were fixed on the dog. "There have been too many times he has barked late," he said. "I cannot understand it."

"The *liona* is cunning, Laxague," the herder said defensively. "It was a full week before I myself knew that he was trailing the herd."

Jean Baptiste remembered the day when he had cut track through the sagebrush foothills in search of the missing lambs. When he had stumbled upon the lion's tracks, he had accepted the loss of the lambs philosophically. To lose to the things of the wild was to be expected. He had merely noticed that his own broad hand could not cover the print, whistled in surprise, and then returned to the herd.

But the weeks that had followed bore proof of a terrible truth, Jean Baptiste remembered bitterly. For the lion had not left the herd to hunt afield. He had trailed the sheep relentlessly. He had become that dreaded thing of the mountains—the herd stalker.

Laxague had returned his attention to his plate. With a thick piece of crust, he scooped up the remainder of the *omeletta*. Then, wiping his hands on his Levi's, he reached for the *chahakoa*. Holding the goatskin pouch aloft in his two hands, he squirted a long drink of wine into his mouth. When he was finished, he wiped his hands on his Levi's again and settled into a position of despondency.

"Batista," he said finally. "I must do something. With the way it is going, I will be lucky if there are enough lambs left to pay your summer wage. It is a terrible thing."

There was a flushed expression of helpless frustration about Laxague's eyes, and his mouth was thin, bitter, and hard.

"Perhaps the *liona* will leave the herd," Jean Baptiste said hopefully. Seeing Laxague discouraged was making him uncomfortable. He was not concerned over his summer wage. He understood that the lion's forays were taking a terrible toll of Laxague's lambs. And because he liked the man, and saw what the weeks of helplessness were doing to him, he had tried in his own way to help. He had made no mention of a new jacket, of pack bags, or a blanket for the jenny. Perhaps his sacrifice was not much, Jean Baptiste thought, but it was his way of helping.

"Bah! There is no chance now," Laxague said bitterly. "He has tasted the blood of the spring lamb. He will stay with us through the whole summer range, sucking the throats and wasting the meat and making me broke. He will not leave us now."

"Can you not find a man with dogs?" Jean Baptiste asked.

"Yes, this week I have heard of one. But he is very expensive. It will cost much. And if he does not find the lion, I will be all the poorer. It is too much of a risk, Batista."

Jean Baptiste shrugged his shoulders and reached for the *cha-hakoa*. Laxague leaned forward and sliced a piece of crust from the sourdough loaf. He lifted it to his mouth and suddenly stopped short, the bread only inches from his lips. His brows were furrowed in thought. He seemed to be trying to remember something.

"Is this the plateau where the wind always blows through the hollow?" he asked, and the hand with the bread was lowered again to the plate.

"Yes," Jean Baptiste answered, gesturing with his hand to the west end of the plateau. "The hollow lies there."

Laxague brought his hand against his knee in a resounding slap. "Batista," he said, "we will make a trap!"

Jean Baptiste regarded him quizzically. "What kind of a trap?"

Laxague's despondency had vanished. His face had suddenly become alight with the expectation of discovery, and he spoke rapidly, excitedly, as the picture took shape in his mind.

"We will stake out a lamb in the brush at the bottom of the hollow, and we will hide above, at the head, where the wind will be always in our faces."

Jean Baptiste interrupted. "But what if the lion chooses to visit the herd instead?"

Laxague's face was triumphant as he answered the question. "We will place lanterns around the herd. How many do you have?" he asked, and then rushed on without waiting for the answer. "I have two in the saddlebags. You have two also, I know. There will be enough kerosene to last the night."

Jean Baptiste accepted the news silently. He had heard of such traps, and most of them had proved unsuccessful. But to say such a thing to Laxague now would not be wise. The man was at his rope's end. And yet, there was a chance. Nowhere in all the Sierra was there such a hollow for a trap. Jean Baptiste stilled the doubts in his mind and said nothing.

At dusk, the two men walked out onto the grassy plateau. Jean Baptiste lifted a curved finger to his mouth and whistled. At the piercing blast, Barbo shot like a furry bolt down the side of the plateau and into the trees. A succession of frantic scurries followed upon the heels of his furious barking, and soon, the whole herd was moving toward the bed ground. The jenny was in the lead, her long ears cocked backward in the direction of the dog, and her bell clanging untunefully in rhythm with her measured gait.

Jean Baptiste threaded his way into the herd and snared a lean lamb, one that he was certain would not do well despite the summer range. He heaved the kicking form to his shoulder and walked toward the hollow.

Descending carefully to the bottom, he found a stout bitter-brush and tied the lamb by a foreleg. Rising, he stood and watched as the lamb struggled to its feet and stared at him bewilderedly. And again, the fury returned to the herder. The thought that this lamb might also die brought a swift, accompanying yearning that the lion would show, that Jean Baptiste could see him once, over the sights of his carbine. There was a score to settle, for the lambs, for Barbo, for Laxague.

The herder turned and surveyed the upper banks of the hollow, noting the many places of concealment in the boulders that flanked one side and in the twisted, jumbled mass of manzanita that covered the other. Behind him, the hollow dipped like the handle of a spoon and emptied downward into the forest. Jean Baptiste nodded to himself. It was as though the hollow had been made to order. He mounted the upper bank and walked swiftly across the plateau, noticing the flickering lights of the lanterns in a circle around the bed ground.

Laxague was waiting for him at the tent. He was bundled in a wool-lined jacket, and the metal of his saddle rifle gleamed dully in the fading light. Jean Baptiste lifted his Levi's jumper from the bed and checked the load in his carbine. He started to turn away and then knelt to rummage through the pack bag for the cartridge box.

Ordering Barbo to remain at the camp, Jean Baptiste strode hurriedly after Laxague's retreating figure. They walked wordlessly to the head of the hollow.

Laxague spoke first. "I will hide on the left side, in the manzanita, and you will take the right side, in the rocks."

Jean Baptiste nodded and moved away, but Laxague halted him with a parting word.

"Batista," he said, "do not become impatient. We will wait the night if it is necessary. And Batista, do not shoot unless you are certain."

Jean Baptiste nodded again and picked his way through the boulders that lined the right side of the hollow. The night was already becoming chilly, and he buttoned the front of the thin jumper.

Behind two boulders that came together so closely that only a small crevice appeared between them, he found a patch of sand and eased himself down. Thrusting the carbine through the crevice, he hunched forward to scan the hollow. The lamb was a patch of gray-white against the dark background of the salt grass and the brush clump. It had ceased to tug at the rope, but its outraged bleats still pierced through the night air.

Jean Baptiste turned his gaze to the left bank of the hollow, where Laxague lay hidden, but the moon was down and he could detect no movement in the mass of blackness that was the manzanita.

Pulling his knees up, he hunkered down into the threadbare warmth of the jumper, marking time by the occasional bleating of the lamb. The night breeze blew in chilling gusts up the hollow and whistled mournfully through the crevice. The heat of the day left the sand on which the herder lay, and the cold penetrated through the thin denim of his clothes. Finally, he stopped lifting his head from the jumper to peer through the crevice. Tucking his hands under his armpits, Jean Baptiste listened as the muffled and lonely bleating of the lamb grew fainter and fainter, and finally faded away.

Jean Baptiste awoke with a grunt, wondering sleepily if he had rolled from his bed. He twisted, felt the crunch of sand beneath him, and knew suddenly that he was in the hollow, that he had fallen asleep. Turning his head, he looked at the sky. The moon was high overhead, and the herder knew he had slept a long time. He turned quickly, peered through the cleft, and breathed in relief when he saw that the hollow was quiet. In the moon's full light, he could see the lamb clearly.

The night had become bitter cold, and Jean Baptiste worked his numbed legs up and down. His hand recoiled from the cold metal of the carbine and he wished desperately for the coming of daylight. He was thrusting his hands inside the lining of the jumper when an alarmed bleat from the hollow jerked him to sudden attentiveness.

Grasping the carbine, he hunched forward and peered through the crevice. The lamb was jerking wildly at the end of the rope, and its shrill bleats were shattering the silence of the night. Then suddenly it fell quiet and stood as if transfixed, staring into the black mass of brush behind the clump to which it was tied.

A twig snapped behind Jean Baptiste, and a cold fear washed through his body. He turned slowly, the hair rising at the nape of his neck. But all was quiet there, and he turned again to the hollow.

Straining forward, he swept the black mass of brush with his gaze, striving to make out what the lamb had seen. Dimly at first, and then clearer, a dark outline took shape before his eyes. Jean Baptiste eased the carbine to his shoulder and searched for the front sight. It swung into line, and his finger tightened on the trigger. Then he remembered Laxague's words, and he eased the pressure, waiting for the dark hulk to move. But it remained maddeningly immobile, and Jean Baptiste lowered the carbine slightly.

As he did so, something gray flashed into his vision and closed with the lamb. But it had come from the wrong direction, from the head of the hollow. Cursing aloud, Jean Baptiste rose to one knee and trained his carbine on the swirling heap. For he could see that the thing that had jumped the lamb was a coyote.

The heavy boom of the carbine rocked the hollow with sound, and the swirling stopped. Jean Baptiste rose to his feet and saw Laxague twisting through the manzanita toward the lamb. Levering the empty cartridge from the chamber, Jean Baptiste made ready to clamber over the boulders. It was then that he heard Laxague's low outcry and looked up.

Poised on the lip of the hollow was the ominous silhouette of the lion. It had been in the brush patch behind him. Jean Baptiste's ears had not deceived him. The cold fascination that filled the herder at the sight was overwhelmed by a sudden, burning surge of frustration.

Snapping the carbine to his shoulder in a lightning motion, he fired blindly as the lion gathered itself for a fleeing leap. Below the roar of the shot, Jean Baptiste heard the bullet hit, heard the lion's scream of rage and pain, and saw the beast collapse on the lip of the hollow.

"He is hit! He is hit!" Laxague shouted as he scrambled through the bitterbrush toward the lion.

"Laxague, look out! Look out!" Jean Baptiste screamed as he saw the lion regain its feet and turn back toward the hollow, snarling furiously at the approaching figure.

Jamming the lever down, Jean Baptiste again whipped the gun to his shoulder and fired at the black hulk on the lip of the hollow.

The lion rose on its hind legs, screaming and clawing the air as the second bullet coursed the width of its back. Then it wheeled away from the hollow and bounded into the darkness. The herder's third shot whined over its head and into the trees.

Jean Baptiste hurdled the boulders and fought his way through the brush to the lip where the lion had fallen, where Laxague now knelt.

"Man, you were lucky," Jean Baptiste gasped out, but Laxague did not hear. He was on his knees in the grass, groping for a match. The light flared in his cupped hands and blew out. Cursing with impatience, Laxague turned his back to the breeze and cupped the flame of a second match. The light flared again, and both of them saw the splashes of blood on the grass.

Laxague rose to his feet. "He is hurt bad," he said. "We will follow him."

"No, Laxague," Jean Baptiste argued. "Let us wait until daylight. It is only a little while. Now, in the darkness, it will be too dangerous. He is mad, Laxague."

Laxague's voice rose in sudden anger. "No, we will follow him now. By daylight, the wounds will heal, and there will be no blood to follow him by. Fetch a lantern from the bed ground."

"But Laxague," Jean Baptiste persisted. "It is insane. We cannot know when he will turn on us in the night."

Laxague's voice was tinged with threat. "We must take that chance. Fetch the lantern, I say."

Jean Baptiste saw that it was useless to argue. The man's reason had been blotted out by his desire to kill the lion. Words would be empty nothings against the wall of the man's emotions. Jean Baptiste shrugged and weaved through the brush to the floor of the hollow, where the lamb had been tied. The coyote was twisting soundlessly in its death agony, and Jean Baptiste watched him without feeling.

But the lamb lay huddled on its side, its breath sobbing in its slashed throat. Jean Baptiste knelt and caught the trembling form in his hands. When he saw that the lamb was dying, he reached for his pocket knife and cut swiftly through the jugular vein. The lamb jerked spasmodically and was still.

"What are you doing?" Laxague called impatiently from the lip of the hollow.

"The lamb, it was suffering," Jean Baptiste answered. When Laxague did not answer, he rose and climbed swiftly out of the hollow and across the plateau. Near the camp, Barbo met him, whining with fear. Jean Baptiste ordered him back to the tent and picked up a lantern. Swishing it back and forth, he made certain that there was enough kerosene to last until daylight, and then he made his way back to the hollow.

Laxague heard his approach and called, "Hurry, Batista. It will be too late."

Jean Baptiste mounted to the lip and held the lantern near the ground. For the first time, they could see the extent of the lion's wounds. Great gobs of blood were splashed in a large circle on the grass.

The two men descended slowly down the outer side of the hollow. Where the lion's first leap ended, they found another great splash of blood. From this, a reddened trail led into the blackness of the forest.

At the edge of the trees, Jean Baptiste halted. Laxague hauled up short and demanded. "What is the matter? Why do you stop?"

"Laxague, I tell you the lion may be waiting for us, perhaps in these trees, perhaps behind a rock or a manzanita bush. It is foolish for both of us to walk along with our heads bent to the trail. One must follow behind and guard the other."

"All right, all right. Give the lantern to me," Laxague said impatiently. "I will follow the trail."

With an apprehensive glance toward the tall pines, Jean Baptiste fell in behind Laxague. They entered into the silent darkness of the forest, Laxague in the fore, his lantern held low to pick up the shiny flecks of blood on the pine needles. Jean Baptiste followed closely behind, his gaze sweeping the circle of light made by the lantern and probing into the darkness beyond. Long minutes had elapsed before he remembered suddenly that the carbine was nearly empty. He fished quickly into the jumper pocket and slipped the cartridges one by one through the loading slot. When the gun was fully loaded, he breathed a sigh of relief.

"He is growing weak, Batista," Laxague whispered hoarsely. "He is slowing up. There is more blood on the needles."

Jean Baptiste did not answer. Directly in the path before them was a low, black shape, barely distinguishable in the outer reaches of the lantern light. Jean Baptiste reached forward quickly and caught Laxague by the skirt of his jacket.

"Laxague, stop!" he called out in a low, strained voice.

Laxague turned to look at him, and it was then that his feet slid on the pine needles and he sprawled on the ground. The lantern clunked loudly on the ground, and the kerosene in the bowl washed upwards, extinguishing the flame. The two men were plunged into utter darkness.

Jean Baptiste dropped to one knee, straining to see the shape. But all was total darkness. The fear surged upward from his stomach and pulled the muscles of his face taut. He waited in tortured silence, uncertain which way to face. Before him, Laxague swore lustily and groped for the lantern. Jean Baptiste heard the scratch of the match and waited with bated breath while Laxague lifted the window of the lantern and touched the match to the wick. When the light flared again, Jean Baptiste bowed his head to his knee and felt the sweat of relief course down from his armpits and trickle across his body. The black shape was still there. It had not moved. It was a log.

"What did you see? Why did you pull me?" Laxague demanded angrily. "Do you jump at every sound?"

"I am sorry, Laxague," Jean Baptiste whispered. "I thought it was something."

"Bah!" Laxague spat out. Swinging the lantern back and forth until he had picked up the trail, he moved forward swiftly. Jean Baptiste followed behind, welcoming the strength that returned slowly to his sapped limbs. By the time they reached the timber's edge, he could speak again.

Now, they were on open ground. The trail was a mottled ribbon in the moonlight, skirting the side of the bare hill. Jean Baptiste looked toward the eastern sky and saw the first gray hint of light outlining the peaks.

Laxague quickened his pace on the bare ground, and soon the two men were shuffling through the sand at a near trot. They topped the bare hill and descended the other side, past the ghostly whiteness of the summer snowbank that lay in the gully. On the edge of the pack, the lion had rested in the snow, and the imprint of his body was lined with red.

From the gully, the trail followed the crest of a high ridge. Laxague whispered excitedly, "Batista, the track is weaving. It will not be long now."

Jean Baptiste nodded silently. His eyes roved unceasingly from side to side. When the trail entered the manzanita thicket, they were forced to claw their way through the clinging branches. They fought their way along slowly, until finally the ridge emptied into the face of the shale mountain.

It was a mountain that Jean Baptiste feared. Great layers of jagged shale rock covered the nearly perpendicular face, seeming to cling miraculously to the mountain itself. Midway across the face, a rickety boulder formation reared its head uncertainly, as if overpowered by the ominous magnificence of the mountain itself.

Jean Baptiste had stood many times where he stood now, shooing adventurous lambs from the threadlike deer trail that crossed the shale face. Once, he had arrived too late. He had watched helplessly as two lambs ventured out upon the trail, and he had seen them attempt to turn around. One had bumped the other playfully, and a slide had started. And as Jean Baptiste looked on, the roaring sheet of shale had carried the lambs to the bottom of the hill. When the dust had cleared, the lambs were nowhere to be seen. They had disappeared from sight.

And now, Jean Baptiste objected vigorously as Laxague moved forward toward the precipitous mountainside. The thin ribbon of blood entered into the opening of the trail. The lion had crossed.

"Laxague," the herder said sharply. "We cannot cross the mountain. We are not deer."

Laxague's voice was even and cold, filled with a deadly determination. "I am too close now to give up," he said. "The lion has crossed the mountain, and so shall I. Come if you wish. If you do not, remain here." Then he turned his back and stepped into the trail.

Jean Baptiste raged inwardly. He had meant to suggest that the two men cross over the top of the mountain and come back from the other side, picking up the lion's track where the trail across the shale face ended. It was not a question of courage, but common sense. But Laxague was without reason now. He would not agree to a plan that would cost even an hour's time, this Jean Baptiste knew. And so, he fell in behind the man. He could not leave him to face the mountain alone.

They crept forward cautiously, their eyes glued to the trail. Once, Jean Baptiste glanced upwards and saw, in the half-light, the sheets of shale that hung over their heads like menacing curtains of death. Steeling himself, he returned his eyes to the trail. So intent was he upon the forward progress of his feet that he did not notice that Laxague had stopped. The collision nearly threw them off balance, down the side of the mountain.

They clung to each other desperately until they had regained their balance. And then, Laxague pointed to the boulder formation that loomed before them.

"Batista, the blood leads into the rocks. He is there, our lion. I swear it."

Jean Baptiste followed the ribbon of blood with his eyes and grunted assent. "How do you propose to bring him out?" he asked.

"One of us must go around," Laxague answered. "We cannot leave the far side open."

Jean Baptiste's decision was sudden. He could not allow Laxague, driven by his unreasoning determination, to fall victim to his own carelessness.

"I will go," Jean Baptiste said quickly, and before Laxague could protest, he grasped the man's shoulders and stepped past him on the trail.

His attention divided between the trail and the looming boulders, Jean Baptiste edged his way slowly past the formation. When he had gained the far side, where the formation rose sheer and high, he knew that he was safe for the moment. Even in its madness, the lion would not attempt a perpendicular leap. Jean Baptiste clung tenaciously to uncertain handholds, pulling himself slowly upwards. When he neared the top, he leaned forward and caught the jutting edge of a rock to pull himself up, and out of the corner of one eye he saw the hindquarters of the lion disappear through the boulders, moving in the direction of Laxague.

"Laxague, look out! Look out!" Jean Baptiste screamed as he leaped forward across the boulder and threw himself toward the near side of the formation. He landed in the shale, his boots digging deeply into the layer of tiny rocks. The leap started it.

Jean Baptiste felt the sheet begin to move beneath him, and he fought wildly to keep his balance, to reach the formation. But he landed on his back in the moving shale, his arms spread-eagled. Glancing down, he saw Laxague's horrified gaze travel first to the shale moving toward him, and then to the lion, crouched on the boulders for a spring.

The shale caught Laxague first, knocking his legs from under him and bowling him downward. The lion landed where Laxague had been, directly onto the moving shale. He scrambled wildly to return to the boulder formation, and then rolled clawing down the side of the mountain.

Steeling himself against the knife-like thrusts of the jagged shale, Jean Baptiste kept his arms and legs rigidly outstretched, coasting on the face of the sheet. Half insensible, he was conscious only of the pain and the choking dust and the roaring in his ears. Below him, in blurred glimpses, he saw Laxague and the lion rolling headlong.

When Jean Baptiste returned to consciousness, his first sensation was of a crushing weight on his legs. Pulling himself to a sitting position, he saw that he had kept hold of the carbine through the descent. He eased his legs painfully from the covering of shale, and then turned on his side to look for Laxague.

The sight that met his eyes through the dusty haze blotted out the pain and the shock that racked his body. Laxague, stunned and bleeding, was fighting to pull himself from the shale that had buried him to the waist. Moving toward the man, its tawny hide torn and matted with blood and dirt, was the lion.

Jean Baptiste twisted quickly over on his stomach and dragged the carbine to his shoulder. Hoping desperately that the barrel had not filled with dirt, that the gun would not explode, he pulled the trigger, even as Laxague looked up through blood-filmed eyes into the snarling face of the lion.

The shot roared against the face of the mountain and clapped back in echo. The bullet crashed into the back of the lion's head, bobbing it with the shock. Its forelegs slid forward awkwardly, and it fell slowly, rolling over on its side. The huge body shuddered convulsively and was still. Jean Baptiste buried his head in his arms to hide the burning tears of relief.

The two men sat side by side on the great pile of shale and watched the morning sun rise in a flaming glory. Its first gentle warmth flooded over them, filling their tired and torn bodies with its promise of strength.

Laxague was the first to move. Rising painfully to his feet, he extended a hand, a trifle self-consciously, to Jean Baptiste. His face, marred by dirt and clotted blood, was strangely peaceful. Impatience and desperation, weariness and frustration, had all been washed away in the long night.

"Come, Batista," he said. "The sheep will be moving. We must return to the camp."

Jean Baptiste took hold of the extended hand and pulled himself to his feet. "The coffee and the *omeletta* will be welcome today, Laxague," he said.

Laxague nodded, and the two men walked toward the forest. They did not look back at the torn and lifeless beast that lay on the mounds of shale.

# VALLEY

## OF

## THE

## DEER

Out of the valleys came the night wind.

Gathering the gusts that tormented the gorges and ravines, it roared up the slopes of the Sierra and flung itself against the massive crag. Then, its fury spent, it sobbed away to the valleys from which it had come.

The camp lay in the saddle between the two ridges, in the shadow of the crag. The tiny tent huddled in the protection of the pines, and before its entrance, the campfire burned stubbornly. The mule stood near the tent, its head bent against the night wind.

Peter Castrow drew his hands from the pockets of the sheepskin jacket and held them to the fire's warmth. His eyes were fixed on the flames, and beneath the stubble of beard, his face was drawn and white. He was dimly aware that Grant Chiles was looking at him again.

"What the hell's eating you, Peter? Why don't you say something?" Grant Chiles's voice was sharp with irritation.

Peter eased his hands into the pockets of the sheepskin jacket. He breathed deeply, his chest heaving with the effort, and he smiled a quick, self-conscious smile. "Sorry, Grant," he said, then paused and added, "Just tired, I guess. It's been a tough climb."

The lines of irritation softened in Grant's face. "There's a tougher one yet to come," he reminded, glancing at the mountain crag that loomed over them. "Don't go getting tired now."

Peter did not follow his gaze, but the drawn tightness returned to his face. He did not look at Grant as he spoke. "I'm getting a little doubtful about that pass. Maybe we ought to hunt to the south and head back to the settlement."

"Why, by God? Why?" demanded Grant perplexedly. "You know damned well we won't see a thing. You said yourself there wasn't a deer in the whole range."

"It's going to be too rough. We might not make it."

"No sir, dammit," cried Grant. "We've come this far and we're going over that pass. If deer can make it, by God, we can."

Peter shrugged and resumed his staring into the flames. Silence fell again over the camp. Above them, the wind wailed helplessly against the unmoving crag. A single gust whirled dervishly downward and snuffed out the fire. Blackness enveloped the camp and Peter gasped sharply.

Scrambling to his knees, he leaned forward and blew furiously into the coals. Fire and light flared again through the camp.

Grant Chiles had heard the gasp, but the irritation that furrowed his brows was mingled now with concern. He asked, almost pleading, "What's the matter, Peter? Back in the city, you were all fired up for this trip. But ever since we reached this country, you've been acting funny."

Peter breathed deeply again, his chest straining beneath the sheepskin jacket. He passed his tongue over dry lips and turned to look at Grant. His voice was flat and exhausted. "Grant, I told you how the deer disappear from these ranges every fall, when the season starts, and how they're supposed to go over the pass into the hidden valley."

"Yeah."

"Well, didn't you wonder, in the settlement down there, why none of the men try the pass?"

"Yeah, I did. But I thought it was because the thing was so steep."

Peter shook his head slowly. "That's not the reason."

"Well, what is it then?"

Peter's shoulders slumped and he turned away from Grant. "Forget it," he muttered. "I'm talking through my hat."

"No, goddam it," Grant cried vehemently. "Tell me! I'm tired of this hocus-pocus."

Peter Castrow heaved for breath again. Without raising his head, he said in a dry, flat monotone, "The old Indians say that during this season, the deer are led over the pass into the valley."

"Led?" Grant asked incredulously.

"Yes."

"By what?"

"By a man. The one the Indians say is the ruler of the hidden valley, the one they call 'the old man of the mountains.'"

"Peter, for Christ's sake! Are you serious?"

Peter Castrow flushed at the incredulity in Grant's voice. "I'm not saying it's so," he said defensively. "It's the legend."

Grant Chiles leaned forward. "Go on."

"That's all. He supposedly keeps them in the valley until the first snows. Then they come down by herds and cross into the desert for the winter."

"Has anyone ever seen the valley?"

Peter nodded. "Yes, even among the Indians, there are some who have seen the valley from the pass. But they have never entered the valley itself."

"Has anyone ever failed to return from the valley?"

Peter Castrow's voice dropped. "When I was a boy, just before I left the settlement, a hunter set out for the valley. He was never seen again."

"Couldn't he have disappeared in any one of a thousand gorges?" Grant persisted.

"Possibly," Peter admitted. "But at any rate, a search party never found any trace of him."

"Did they search the valley?"

"No."

"Why not?"

"They said they didn't want to chance the pass."

"Do you think there was any other reason why they didn't?"

"I don't know," Peter said hesitantly. "I'm not sure."

Grant Chiles leaned forward intently. "Now, answer me this," he demanded. "Has anyone *ever* seen this old man?"

"No," Peter admitted ruefully.

Grant Chiles rocked back on his haunches. "I suppose you realize there's a damned simple explanation to all this."

Peter Castrow spoke hesitantly. "I guess so."

"Guess, hell. Know!" cried Grant. "In any hunting country, the deer head for the high ranges as soon as the season starts, just from plain instinct. This business about your hidden valley is no more of a mystery than that. They've found a good place to hide out. That's all there is to it."

Peter nodded. The flush of embarrassment had again colored his cheeks. "I've told that to myself a thousand times," he said. "But I guess I just needed to have someone else say it." He rose to his feet and stretched. "I'm part Indian, you know. Guess that's why I'm such a pushover for legends."

Grant Chiles laughed and kneeled to scoop shovelfuls of dirt into the fire pit. The two men groped their way toward the tiny tent.

The twisted, ragged face of the great crag reared above them in the grey light of dawn. Like a giant barrier set upon the core of the mountain, it rose until its pinnacle was lost from the men below. Rocks lay slabbed upon rocks in an ever-rising succession, and from the fissures, the starved, gnarled trunks of trees reached out. The trail began and was lost in the knifed crevices that scarred the stone face.

Grant Chiles, his hands on his hips, whistled aloud. "Holy cow! I don't wonder no one ever takes this thing on."

Peter glanced apprehensively at the mule. "I hope she can pull it."

"She better. I can't quite picture myself lugging a buck over this thing," Grant said, stepping into the trail.

Up the raw face of the crag they climbed, clinging to the tortuous trail, pulling and shoving the wheezing mule through the narrow clefts, scrambling for balance in the loose rubble that marked the ascents from one great slab to another.

As they mounted higher, they stopped often to rest, their chests rising and falling in the thin, unrelieving air. They had shed their jackets, and still their shirts clung heavy with sweat to their limbs.

Grant studiously avoided staring over the side of the crag. "Heights scare the hell out of me," he gasped. "I don't know what the hell I'm doing here."

Finally, the twin columns that flanked the pass loomed above them. Peter stopped short on the trail, his face tight beneath the gray of exhaustion. "I think we better give it up," he said hoarsely. "This is too rough."

Grant turned at the words. "Peter," he said reprovingly. Peter lowered his eyes to the trail and they mounted nearer the twin columns.

On the trail's last turn across the face of the crag, they pressed themselves to the stone as the wind fought to tear them free. The screaming gusts muted their gasps, nearly blinding them with its fury. But then, as they inched their way past the final turn, they were in the narrow pass, and the wind was only a wailing from without.

They stood wordlessly, gazing downward into the valley ahead. Mountainsides covered with manzanita sloped sharply down from the jagged rock barriers that rimmed the valley. Forests of fir, the thickest they had ever seen, lined the foot of the mountain, and within their protecting rim lay the floor of the valley.

Green meadows, hazily brilliant in the light of the morning sun, were lined with streams that shone like silver veins in the sunlight. And in the meadows they saw the deer, roaming in herds through the deep grass. Over the valley hung an immense silence.

Grant Chiles, his voice washed clean of exhaustion, beckoned Peter as they began the swift descent. But Peter stood rigidly on the crest of the trail, staring downward to the valley.

"For Christ's sake, Peter. Come on," Grant called curtly. Peter fell in silently behind the mule.

At the edge of the forest of firs, they unlimbered their rifles from the scabbards hanging from the packsaddle. Suddenly, with a startled crash, a buck bounded from the firs. It stood before them, poised briefly in naked outline against the forest.

"Your shot, Peter," Grant cried excitedly.

Peter jerked the rifle to his shoulder. His finger tightened on the trigger, then relaxed. As he lowered the rifle, the buck wheeled into the trees.

Cursing aloud, Grant fired wildly at the bounding deer. The shots crashed through the silence of the valley in an outrage of sound.

Grant Chiles's face was distorted with fury as he turned to face Peter. "All my life, I've dreamt of a shot like that," he cried. "I'm not going to ask you what's the matter. It would only make me sick to my stomach." He turned away. "Come on, goddamn it. We're getting that buck."

Looping the mule's tether rope around the root of a manzanita bush, he ran toward the forest. Peter hesitated momentarily, then fell in behind.

Sunlight faded into gloom under the canopy of the firs. They fought their way forward blindly through the branches that blocked their path at every turn. Somewhere before them, they could hear the deer's frightened dash. They plunged on, raising their arms before them to block the tearing limbs of the firs.

Then, as suddenly and overwhelmingly as it had begun, the forest ended and they stood in a great clearing. Before them, by the shattered trunk of a tree, was the buck. Grant Chiles dropped quickly to one knee and raised the rifle to his shoulder.

"Don't shoot! Don't shoot!" shouted Peter Castrow, even as the shot thundered through the clearing. The buck recoiled from the impact of the bullet. It reared once, the blood welling from the gaping hole in its neck, and then it fell violently on its side.

Grant Chiles leaped to his feet exultantly. He turned to face Peter, and as he did, the smile faded from his face.

Peter was on his knees and his face was as the face of death. His eyes were fixed in horror before him, and from his lips came muffled sobs. Grant Chiles wheeled to follow his stare.

There, in the clearing trampled bare by the prints of a thousand hooves, stood the trunk of a tree, a trunk shaped like a throne. It loomed over the clearing like the chair of a monarch.

Grant Chiles fought to lift Peter to his feet.

"Peter, Peter," he cried. "It's not what you think, man! It was done by lightning. I've seen dozens like it. Dozens, I tell you!"

Peter rose, his frame shuddering. Grant Chiles turned him toward the forest. "Go back and get the mule, Peter," he begged. "We'll load this one up and get out of here. We'll be out of here in no time. Hurry up, please!"

Peter moved forward a few steps and watched as Grant Chiles hurriedly leaned his rifle against the great trunk and moved towards the deer. Then he turned and stumbled into the forest.

Groping his way woodenly through the thick gloom, he found the mule and began the return. And then suddenly, with a terrible finality, there was another shot. He listened as the echoes clapped against the valley walls, and then he burst forward blindly, jerking the mule behind him.

He found Grant Chiles sprawled beside the deer. In the numbing haziness that flooded his mind, he saw the blood that seeped from the hole in the man's head, and he saw the rifle, where it had toppled from the trunk.

Peter Castrow stood stock-still and listened as the silence fell again over the valley. Then his eyes fastened again on the rifle and he ran toward it. But even as his fingers groped for the stock, he recoiled and stepped back, raising his empty hands before him.

At the base of the trail, he stopped the mule and tightened the ropes that held the body to the packsaddle.

"I told you. I told you," he said. "It was your own fault, you know."

# FORMERLY,

## ANY

## QUADRUPED

Far be it from me to be a spoiler of myths. Under ordinary circumstances, I am as willing as the next man to subscribe to the preservation of all sorts of legendary nonsense, if only to maintain sanity in an otherwise humdrum existence. Some of my happiest hours have been spent contemplating such fictions as the one about hard work bringing fortune, that everything happens for the best, or in my more fanciful moments, that politicians are finally squaring with the public.

But these are myths, designed to soothe the soul along the road to old age and enlightenment. They never really harm anyone except to weave another link in life's daisy chain of disillusionment, which got started at about the time we saw Santa Claus taking a belt of whiskey in the kitchen when he came visiting on Christmas Eve.

However, it's one thing to be an observer of myths. It's quite another to be an accomplice in their perpetuation, and this is exactly what I have become. I am living a lie.

At first, I imagined that when the symbol of my deed—the bloody carcass hanging in its gauze shroud from a rafter in the garage—had been disposed of, the whole affair would be forgotten. But I did not reckon with either my son or the contagious stuff of myths.

I realize now how indelible is his recollection of the night I came home from my hunting trip after deer in northern Nevada. I should have known from the roundness of his eyes and his breathless cries of, "Mommy, Mommy! Come and see. Daddy shot a *deer!*" And if that weren't enough, I should certainly have known from the awe in his face when he regarded his usually citified father in rumpled, dusty clothes and boots, with a stubble of beard, and smelling of sagebrush and raw whiskey.

I didn't mind the impression I had created. In fact, I rather enjoyed it. I had assumed a new identity that lifted me from the ranks of the faceless ciphers that walk the city streets. But now that I am back at my desk and home and yard, I yearn for a return to my former slovenly habits. I can no longer shuffle about the house. For the benefit of the children that my son brings home to gaze at me in awe, I have to squint as from long habit of staring into wind and sun, and walk with the silent, grim demeanor of the hunter.

I am tired of people calling me for advice about guns that I never even knew existed, newspaper editors hounding me to write columns with such titles as "News Notes for Nimrods," and requests from hunting-clubs for lectures on my life and times in the wilds. And at the office, I am tired of being known affectionately as "Old Leatherstocking."

In a word, I am going to clear my conscience. I am going to make a confession, let the chips fall where they may. I have sinned, but the guilt is not all mine, not by a long shot. I have also been made the pawn of an even greater sin. And if after hearing my story, my son does not have charity in his heart, he had better get it soon, or get out.

Once upon a time, not so very long ago, a person whom I considered my friend came to the house one evening as I was doing the bills. I mention this latter because it was psychologically important to my decision. After trying hopelessly to balance income against expenses, I was engaged in my favorite pastime of indulging in a myth, namely that the only answer was a return to the simple life.

My friend burst in on me with what I can only describe as animal good spirits. Since I had regarded him with kinship as one of retiring and studious nature, I was startled by his appearance, since he was dressed in plaid shirt, khaki trousers, and boots, and wore a long knife on his belt. He strode to the center of the floor, planted himself there with legs apart and hands on hips, and announced, "Pardner, git yore gear. We're a goin' huntin'!"

For a moment, I was too surprised to say anything. In fact, I am afraid I was watching him suspiciously from behind my spectacles. "What are you going to do with that knife?" was all that I could manage.

"Skin the antlered stag," he cried. Whipping the gleaming blade from its sheath, he pointed south. "I'm serious," he said. "We're going north, hundreds of miles out into the wilderness, far from cities and towns, into the greatest deer country in the world!"

I was fascinated. As he sped along with glowing descriptions of crisp, cold mornings and bold, warming draughts of whiskey, of the steaming, old-fashioned country breakfasts at the ranch house where we would headquarter, of the hunt along the primitive trails where the great herds of Idaho deer migrated by the thousands into Nevada, I was spellbound. With pleasure and horror, I realized that my nostrils were flaring from what I knew must be the blood lust of the hunter.

My emotion must have transmitted itself, because he suddenly let off and looked at me apprehensively. "You can shoot, can't you?"

"Well, I have shot," I said lamely.

"Ah! A sharpshooter, eh?" he said, taking the opposite tack. "Don't have to be worried about you!" With that remark, the first gray thought crossed my mind: did I have to be worried about *him?* But of course that was foolish. Obviously he was an accomplished hunter.

His elation cooled once again when we went into the matter of equipment. "You do have a deer gun?" he asked.

"No."

"Sleeping bag?"

"No."

"Canteen?"

"No."

"What the hell do you have?"

"Just myself," I said with an embarrassed little laugh.

"Well, I guess it will have to do," he said, not very graciously. "You can use my wife's gear."

"Is she a hunter, too?" I asked incredulously, the image of his slender, poised wife holding a cocktail glass rising before me.

"Of course," he said with disdain.

"I never knew this side of your character."

"There are more things in heaven and earth, Horatio, than are dreamed of in your philosophy," he said.

At the moment, I didn't think his remark appropriate. But as things turned out, it was certainly prophetic.

I'm not certain why, but there seems to be a rule among deer hunters that they must rise to the hunt before daylight, at 4 A.M. to be precise, whether they are hunting that day or not, or as in our case, merely driving to our destination in northern Nevada. But being caught up in the spirit of the thing, rise I did, leaving my warm bed and groping my way through the darkness to the curb, where punctual George awaited me a little grumpily. For some reason, he had expected me to be waiting in the dark at the street.

I came awake in a hurry, however, because as soon as I was within reach, he thrust a cold rifle into my hands. "Here," he said. "Elaine says you're welcome to use her rifle." I mumbled my thanks, and then he had to go and say, "But she says be sure to come back with some blood on it."

I couldn't help it. For one thing, it was too early in the morning. And I could have sworn I felt something sticky under my fingers. I dropped the gun. With an oath and some smothered muttering about hand-crafted weapons and tenderfeet, George retrieved it and eased it into the back of the jeep. We were on our way!

The first leg of our journey took us from my house on the outskirts of Reno to a gambling casino which was just downtown. "Why are we stopping here?" I asked. It seemed to me a reasonable question.

George sighed impatiently. "To register for the deer contest, of course."

I shrugged. "You go ahead. It would be a waste of time for me. I'm not that good of a hunter."

"You don't have to shoot a deer to win," said George shortly.

"Then why do they call it a deer contest?"

George was a little flustered. "I don't know," he said. "I understand they changed the rule one year when the hunting was pretty lean. But don't ask me. That's their business."

George was right. There in bold, black letters on the registration form were the words, "You Do Not Have to Shoot a Deer to Win." Still a little uncomprehending as we walked out of the club, I looked at the duplicate form that had been given to me for a receipt. It contained an impressive list of prizes. I scanned them quickly. "Well, that's odd," I remarked. "Did you ever see such a curious collection of prizes for a deer contest? Badminton sets, golf clubs, skin diving outfits—"

George was reaching the limits of his patience. He stopped and faced me. "Listen," he said. "Don't ask so many naive questions. You lower yourself in stature when you do. Everybody will think you're a tenderfoot, and that's unforgivable."

I let it go and for George's sake promised him that I would ask no more questions. After all, he was taking me on a new experience, and I didn't want to embarrass him in any way.

The second leg of our journey was to a restaurant on the other side of town. It advertised special breakfasts for deer hunters. Still a little queasy from my experience about bloody guns, I ordered straight coffee. But as time wore on and George didn't seem to be the least inclined to leave, I recovered my appetite and had breakfast. As we sat, I noticed that the restaurant was filled with plaid shirts and khaki trousers, all the wearers of which seemed disinclined to leave, but were whiling away their time drinking coffee and regaling each other with hearty tales of deer-hunting exploits. Listening to them, I began to feel the warm camaraderie of the hunter.

Daylight had come and gone and the sun was well up in the heavens when George finally got to his feet and announced, "Well, let's go gettum big buck!"

At his words, several of the hunters turned to regard us with friendly curiosity, and, it seemed to me, no little surprise. One of them detached himself from the counter and came over to us. "Where you aimin' to go, fellers?" he asked with a twang.

"Up Badger Creek way, in northern Nevada," said George.

The hunter shook his head enviously. "That's the finest deer country in the world," he said, lapsing into correct English. "You'll get some big ones up there. That's the migratory route for those great herds of Idaho deer, you know."

"Yes, we know that," George said quickly before I could make a comment.

"Wish I could join you," the hunter said. "I've had some great times up there."

"Where you going?" I asked in what I thought was a carefully couched question.

"Oh, just in the country hereabouts," the hunter said. "None of our bunch at the office can get any vacation right now, so we try and get in a few hours hunting before it's time for work." With that, he looked at his watch. "By gosh, it's almost that time now. Guess I better get home and change my clothes, or else I'll be late again."

I almost said something, but then I perceived George staring at me with apprehension. So I only nodded and smiled in goodbye. George was still a little wary after we had gotten into the car, but when he realized that I was not going to bring up the subject, he grinned at me in friendship and fatherly pride.

The third leg of our journey was considerably longer. George had not been speaking idly when he said it was hundreds of miles, and north. Because north we went, hour after hour after hour, through mountain ranges and deserts, with the towns getting smaller and smaller, until there were no towns at all, and finally, not even a paved highway. I had never considered myself particularly attached to asphalt before, but when we turned off onto our first dirt road, I began to realize how deep a place it had in my affections.

The dirt road, or what we could see of it, wound interminably through sagebrush and desert hills. There was not a sign of habitation anywhere, nor had there been for the last two hours. I began to feel forlorn. "You're sure you know where you're going?" I asked George, seeking reassurance.

"Durned tootin' I know where I'm a goin'," said George. "I know this country like my own back yard."

This did not particularly reassure me, because the last time we were visiting at his home, he couldn't remember where the turnoff valve was for the sprinkling system, although he had been using it for the past five years. Still, I had to marvel at the certainty with which he weaved through the confusing network of unmarked dirt roads. That is, until we came to a place where the road simply ended in a swamp.

We sat in strained silence, contemplating the swamp. "Guess our road petered out on us," said George with a nervous laugh. It was an expression with which I was to become all too familiar in the hours to come. When I said nothing, he went on defensively. "I'm certain it's one of the main roads to the ranch, but obviously, the beaver have flooded it out."

"Beaver!" I said. "I thought they went out with the Hudson's Bay Company."

"Don't be ridiculous," he said loftily. "This is also the great migratory route for the beaver from Idaho. Can't you see their dam up there?"

I took a second look at the big mound at the end of the swamp. It still looked like a pile of twigs and branches that had been washed down by the creek, but he sounded so convincing that I gave him the benefit of the doubt. We turned the jeep around and retraced our route to the last intersection.

If it were possible, I became more hopelessly lost in the next few hours than before. With a sure hand, George took right and left turns at a hundred crossroads without even the slightest hesitation. I did not question him, but remembering that he had told me once that the ranch was sixty miles from the main highway, I surreptitiously kept tabs on the odometer. By a few hours after nightfall, we had traveled exactly one hundred miles since last we left the asphalt.

Finally, with the last of our strength and gasoline ebbing, we rounded a hill and saw a light in the distance. "Funny," said George. "I don't remember a ranch right here. Must be a new homestead," he concluded, savoring the word.

When we came to the gate, we could see dimly that some letters had been carved into a board nailed to the side post. We got out of the jeep and George shined his flashlight on the board. "Badger Creek Ranch," he said slowly, trying to make out the words. Then, before he could check himself, he exclaimed with the elation of an Admiral Byrd. "I'll be damned! We're here."

I patted him on the back and said admiringly, "I just don't see how you did it."

George shrugged. "Aw, it's either born in you or it ain't." But by then, I had learned the hunter's virtue of silence, and so I said nothing.

It was a while before George succeeded in making his good friend, Ben the rancher, recollect him enough to let us in the front door. But perhaps it may have been by reason of his language, because whatever was left of George's good English went to hell in a basket then and there. As soon as the door was opened, George waved his arm in a wide arc and shouted across the intervening three feet, "Wal, howdy, ol' Ben! It's shore good t'see ye and this hyer country, too. If I had muh druthers, this hyer is where I'd rest muh bones for keeps."

As hard put as I was to understand what George was saying, it occurred to me that Ben the rancher was even more so. With mouth slightly ajar, he regarded George in silence for a long time. Then recognition finally dawned, and he said, "Oh, I remember you now. You're one of those fellows from the city. What're you doing up here?"

"We come to gettum big buck!" shouted George.

Incomprehension fell over Ben's features again. Then he said, "Oh, I get what you mean. Good grief, is it that time of year again?" Recovering himself quickly, he said, "Well, you're sure welcome to stay here as long as you want."

Only slightly daunted, George said, "Thanks, ol' pardner. You can count on us rustling ourselves out at four o'clock. A.M."

"Four o'clock!" said Ben, shaken up again. "Oh, I remember now. You deer hunters like to get an early start."

George was strangely silent as we unrolled our sleeping bags and crawled in. But I was too cold to care anyway, because that night the temperature dropped out of sight. By 4 A.M., my face was encased in ice and there was no sensation of life in my limbs. This was somewhat unfortunate in that when I woke up and heard Ben grumbling in the kitchen about the fact that deer must like to sleep, too, I smiled maliciously, and my lips cracked in twenty places.

I had to hand it to George, however. He was a dedicated hunter, because by 4:30 A.M., we were standing outside and ready to go. After explaining to us where not to hunt because of his livestock, Ben had unexpectedly decided to come along. Bleakly holding my rifle, I was watching George tinker with the jeep when I realized he was taking the top off. "Just why are you doing that, George?" I asked incredulously.

George laughed with a patronizing air. "What's the matter, pardner? Be ye afraid of a little cold air?"

Though it was a point to be considered, I said, "No. But if this is the migratory route for those great herds of Idaho deer, we could get trampled."

"I don't think that's very funny," said George.

However, my remark had been as much in earnest as in jest, and I was about to tell him so when Ben was suddenly seized with such a nasty fit of coughing that George was obliged to haul out a bottle of whiskey and give him a drink. Then, for our own protection, we each had one, too.

It was fortunate that George had had the foresight to bring whiskey along, because the icy morning air was obviously affecting Ben. As we bounced along the dirt road from the ranch, I noticed that a number of fence posts were graced with the whitened skulls of what I took to be horses and cattle. Out of curiosity, I raised the question with Ben. He began to tremble grimly. As though anticipating another seizure, George handed him the bottle quickly and, as Ben was drinking, muttered something to me about hard winters and frozen livestock. In my condition, this was readily understandable. I nodded vigorously and reached for the bottle as soon as Ben was done.

When our road petered out on us, and we proceeded on foot over the trail to the water hole where we were to stand vigil, I had cause to regret my earlier remark to George. Trampled into a veritable highway, the trail was quite formidable and the fresher of the hoofprints were every bit as large as those made by Ben's cattle around the ranch house. I pointed this out to George, but again he received me in bad grace. Lingering behind Ben for a moment, he said, "You're doing two things wrong. You're talking when you should be keeping your eye out for deer. And you're asking questions again."

Chastened by this rebuke, I proceeded the rest of the way to the water hole in stoical silence, and in an effort to regain George's good graces, did so on the balls of my feet. It was painful going, but it did the trick. With an approving smile, George motioned me to my station in a grove of trees overlooking the water hole. With rifle at the ready, I stood there on the alert until George and Ben retrieved me an hour later. I had seen nothing, and neither had they. Apparently, the deer were not drinking water that day. Mulling over the pros and cons of mentioning this observation to George and Ben, I could see nothing wrong in it, but decided against it, anyway. Somehow, everything I said seemed to be wrong.

By the time we reached the jeep, the sun was peeping over the horizon. However, its rays were not strong enough to warm us after our chilled stand, and so George brought out the bottle of whiskey again. We had almost finished it when George, who had occasionally been gazing through his telescope rifle at the distant horizon, suddenly yelped. "Thar they be!" he cried. "Lordy, there must be a hundred of 'em!"

With heart pounding, I leaped unsteadily to my feet and looked wildly around. "Where, where, where?"

George handed me my rifle. "Thar yonder, leapin' an jumpin' over the sagebrush! Ye can see 'em through yore scope."

And see them I did, through the telescope, though they were so tiny that they resembled myriad dancing spots against the sky-line. Staring at them until I had had my exultant fill, I lowered the rifle. To my surprise, I could still see them, and much more clearly than I could see George, though he was standing next to me. It occurred to me then that the combination of open air and raw whiskey had by some strange chemistry made me farsighted.

Conducting himself with admirable reserve in spite of his excitement, George herded us into the jeep, though Ben mumbled that he would just as soon sleep where he was on the ground for a while. With motor roaring, we sped joltingly along in pursuit of the great herd.

It was no easy task, however. For a while, every road we took sooner or later petered out on us, and Ben for the life of him could not seem to remember which road went where. Finally, we abandoned them all and blazed our own trail. With George driving and yipping us on, we traversed the caprocks (rocks on top of a hill), swales (indentations in the terrain), hollows (much like a swale), barrancas (long indentations in the terrain), and arroyos (very much like a barranca).

Finally, as we neared the place where we had seen the deer, George stopped the jeep and we checked our rifles. George was beside himself. "No jackrabbits for us today," he chortled to my utter confusion, until I realized he meant small deer. "No siree. We'll go home with bucks packin' racks like rockin' chairs."

Fortifying ourselves with long pulls from a new bottle of whiskey and urging an unwilling Ben along with us, we crept to the crest of the hill and looked over. Below, there was a grove of quaking aspen trees that offered the only cover for miles around.

"Oh Lordy," George moaned. "They be hidin' in them quakies, all right." With narrowed eyes, he outlined our plan of attack. He and Ben would take to the right side of the quakies, and I to the left. At a given hand signal, we would all throw rocks into the trees. If the startled deer bolted to the right, it was to be George's shot; if to the left, mine. Noting that even Ben was listening in open-mouthed excitement, I nodded silently so as not to betray my own emotions. Stealthily, we parted company and descended the hill.

When I reached the grove, I was forced to wait in position for a time, since Ben was experiencing some difficulty in getting down to flat ground. Finding a rock that I could manage to throw, I nervously awaited George's hand signal. When it finally came, I threw the rock with all my might, and it actually reached the trees.

After the prolonged silence, the sound of the rocks crashing through the branches was deafening. But it was nothing to compare with what followed. Right on the heels of the sound, there was a surprised grunt and a thundering rumble of hooves that struck dread to my heart.

"He's coming your way," George shouted, almost in a scream. "Shoot him! Shoot him!"

With transfixed limbs, I turned helplessly to look at George. He was jumping up and down in great agitation. Then I saw that Ben was beside himself, too. "Shoot, you durned fool! Shoot!"

So I shot. Woodenly raising my rifle to a semblance of position, I saw through swimming vision an awesome hulk bearing down on me, and I shot. Mingled with the deafening roar of the gun, there was a loud bellow and a jarring thump and a cloud of dust as my buck hit the ground.

Above the ringing in my ears, I heard George's yelps of delight as he and Ben ran toward me. But Ben had something else to say about it. "You damned fool," he cried. "You've killed my prize heifer!"

On our long trip back to the highway, George repeated his earlier performance of trial and error, but it didn't seem to matter anymore. My mind was possessed only with the marbled mass of meat wrapped in white gauze in the back seat.

"I would just as soon have left the meat with Ben," I said, breaking the silence. "Over a few months, I could probably manage to cover up the money part of it in the bank account. But how can I ever explain to my family and friends that I shot a cow?"

George had been humming merrily. "Nothing to it, old pardner."

"I would like to know what you mean by that," I said testily. It was easy for him to be flip. He hadn't shot a cow.

"Tell them it's venison," he said airily.

"Don't be funny," I said. "They'll know it isn't venison."

"How?" he said. "Have they ever tasted venison?"

"Well, no," I said. "How could they?"

"You're beginning to get the idea," said George.

And there it was. Now, I knew everything. Now, I knew why I had never known anyone who had tasted venison, why You Do Not Have to Shoot a Deer to Win badminton sets and skin diving outfits, why I had spent so much fruitless time looking to right and left at the Watch for Deer signs on the highways, when there was no such animal, because it was a hoax gleaned from the mythical exploits of Robin Hood, who was more than a little mythical himself, perpetuated by the sporting goods stores and *Field and Stream* magazine and the hunter's virtue of silence, which is in reality a conspiracy of silence, and protected by such dedicated followers as George, who, knowing full well what was going through my mind, could still look out over a landscape in which there was no living thing, and say to me, "When bird season comes around, we'll have to make another trip up here. This is the greatest chukar country in the world, you know."

I don't know what a chukar is. But one thing I do know. I'll never find out.

# WINE

The boy rose from the table and walked to the kitchen stove, running his fingers through his short-cut hair in quick, nervous movements.

"Dammit, Mom," he cried. "Can't you see what it's doing to him?"

The mother arched a fleshy arm over the stove and tested the boiling potatoes with an experimental jab of her fork. Her stern features softened in a disarming smile.

"Now, Peter," she murmured. "You're making a big fuss over nothing. He's getting along perfectly well without it."

The boy clenched his hands helplessly. "But he's not getting along 'perfectly well.' Christ, he looks like a ghost."

The mother shook her head disapprovingly. "Now, don't swear, Peter. He's just getting old, that's all."

"Sure he's getting old, but you're helping him get there faster than he ought."

The mother replaced the lid on the boiling potatoes. "You're just making a big fuss over nothing," she murmured. "Now, why don't you sit down and drink your coffee?"

The boy lingered undecided by the stove for a moment, then he turned and retraced his steps to the table. He was tall, with the vanishing gangliness of adolescence, and there was a shaving rash high on his throat. He fumbled with the package of cigarettes and jerked one loose.

"It's good to have you home again, Peter," she murmured. "I get awfully lonesome around here sometimes." She paused to pour more coffee into the cup on the kitchen table. "Why don't you tell me about school?"

The boy touched a match to his cigarette, then waved out the flame with a jerk of his hand. "The hell with school. This is important, dammit. Can't you realize that?"

The mother sighed wearily, and her face assumed an expression of long-suffering. "Now, I don't wan't to talk about it anymore. Let's just leave it alone."

The boy slammed his clenched fist down on the table. The cup and saucer jangled, and coffee waved over the sides. Anger flared into the mother's eyes.

"You watch your temper, boy. You just watch your temper. You hear me?"

The boy let his hand slide from the table into his lap. "I'm sorry. I didn't mean to do that. But Mom, you've just got to see reason." He paused and was silent for a moment. Then he leaned forward. "What did the doctor say about it?"

"I haven't asked him," the mother said defensively, the anger fading from her voice.

The boy rose to his feet again. "You're afraid to ask him. You know damned well he'd say there's nothing wrong with it. I bet he'd even tell you it's dangerous, what you're doing."

The mother shook her head. "I doubt that very much. Wine never helped anyone."

"Maybe not, but in his case, it's hurting him to take it away."

"I'm glad you admitted it never helped anyone."

The boy's face twisted. "Oh, for Christ's sake, Mom. Why do you always take half of what I say? Can't you see he was practically weaned on wine in the old country? He's had wine with his dinners ever since he's been able to walk. And now that he can't walk, you cut him off cold."

"He's never said a word about it. Never, not once."

The boy stuffed the cigarette out in the ashtray, twisting it angrily. "No, and you know why? Because he knows what you're thinking and he's got too much pride to beg. That's why."

The mother shook her head in the same, knowing movement. "That's not true at all. Everyone has to beg sometime in his life."

"But not Pop. Maybe everyone else, but not Pop. He's never begged for anything."

The disarming smile returned to the mother's lips. "Now, Peter. I've known your father much longer than you."

"Maybe you've known him longer," the boy said evenly. "But you've never known him."

The mother pondered the words for a moment. "Now, I can't make sense out of that at all."

The boy turned away and returned to his chair by the table. "Forget it," he muttered. He stared unseeingly at the cup of coffee. "God, he's gotten older in this last six months than in the last five years."

The mother patted the meat chops down on the crumb-covered breadboard. "It's God's will, Peter. There's nothing we can do about it."

The boy's eyes grew hot again. "Maybe it's God's will, all right. But there's sure something we can do about it. Give him back his wine." He leaned forward across the table. "Would you please tell me how much damage one little glass of wine at dinner can do to anyone?"

"Liquor never helped anyone," the mother said.

"But it's not liquor. I mean . . ." The boy's hands clenched helplessly again, and then he relaxed them. "Forget it," he muttered. "Forget it."

The silence of the kitchen was marked with the sound of the meat slapping gently against the breadboard. The boy stared emptily at the floor. "He looks like a ghost," he muttered. "God, he just looks like hell."

The mother glanced up from her work. "Dinner's going to be ready in a few minutes. You better tell your father to get ready."

The boy's brows were furrowed thoughtfully. He rose from the table and left the kitchen. The mother placed the chops in the pan, and a warm sizzling filled the kitchen. She raised one finger and placed it on her lips meditatively, and then opened the refrigerator door. As she closed it, the boy banged through the kitchen door excitedly. He stood before her, smiling triumphantly.

"I've got news for you. I just phoned the doctor, and you know what he said? He said a little wine wouldn't hurt him a damned bit with his meals."

The mother blinked her eyes rapidly. Then her lips set stubbornly. "Doctors don't know everything."

The boy smashed his clenched fist into the palm of his hand. "That does it. That does it. Hell, I'm not going to argue anymore. The hell with it. That's what I say." He turned away and moved rapidly toward the door. "But I'll be damned if I'm going to sit through dinner and watch that torture, watch him pick at his food and eat nothing. I'm going downtown to eat."

The mother's face flushed concernedly. "Peter," she called as the boy pulled open the door.

He turned in the doorway. "Yes?"

The mother was silent for a moment, and then she spoke, slowly. "If it's that important to you, and if the doctor says it's all right, then I guess it wouldn't do him any harm to have just a little glass with his meals."

As the mother was speaking, the anger disappeared from the

boy's face. "Mom, that's wonderful," he cried excitedly. "That's just goddam wonderful. You won't regret it." He turned into the kitchen, then turned again and pulled open the door. "I'm going to ask him what kind he wants. Then I'll hop over to the store. It'll only take a minute."

When the door had swung shut behind the boy, the mother turned the chops over with her fork. She lifted the steaming potatoes from the pot and heaped them in a dish. A puzzled expression crossed her face as she heard the sound of slow footsteps in the dining room. The kitchen door opened slowly and the boy entered. He closed it quietly and stood leaning against it, his eyes stunned.

"What's the matter, Peter?" the mother asked.

"He doesn't want any," the boy said and his voice was empty. "He doesn't want any. He says he can get along without it."

# THE

---

# GRADUATION

The measured strains of the Coronation March rose uncertainly and then with increasing confidence from the band box below the stage, stilling the sea of whispers that filled the auditorium. The double doors at the rear of the room swung open, and the flowing blue and white line of high school graduates moved with practiced pace down the aisle. There was a general shuffling of feet on the polished floor as a thousand faces turned expectantly.

Some of the graduates in the line marched with an air of assumed dignity, as though looking down from a great height, while others, especially the girls, fought to control mouths that threatened to curve upwards in grins unbecoming to the solemnity of the occasion.

Everywhere along the line, sidelong glances were cast into the crowd in secretive search for parents or friends. But Joseph walked with his eyes fixed painfully forward, his face drawn, showing nothing but his desperate effort to show nothing. Quite without being aware of it, he was vividly conspicious in the line.

As he neared the roped section reserved for parents of the graduates, he was suddenly fearful that his mother would call out. Yes, it would have to be his mother. She was that way. His father was too withdrawn to make a sound. At the thought, Joseph felt the flush rising on his neck. He fought to banish it, but in fighting, he felt it all the more. The march past the roped section was without incident, but by the time the graduates mounted the steps and circled through the darkness of the wings, Joseph's face was scarlet. He felt a flooding relief in the darkness, but it was too brief. He had hardly tasted it when he was again in the glaring light, this time on the stage.

As the graduates in the rear of the line trooped to their places, Joseph stood before his seat in the front row. He was little more than short, with heavy black hair and a face strangely thin and tortured. His eyes were set deep and black in flushed hollows, and his lips were thin and nervous. As he stood, he averted his eyes from the faces below, knowing that two of those faces would be watching only him. Instead, he fixed his gaze on the speaker's stand, but the stand, the water pitcher, and the glass swam dizzily in his vision. The minister began to intone the prayer in a voice dramatic and conscious only of the words he spoke, and Joseph bowed his head with the others and closed his eyes. Again, there was a relief in the darkness, but it too was short-lived.

When they were all finally seated and her elbow was touching his in the concealed folds of the graduation robes, he became poignantly aware of Valerie's presence. There was comfort in the touch, but the comfort was mingled with desire, almost a desperate desire to cling to her. Not actually to cling to her, for he knew that could never be, but a desire at least to be near her.

At the speaker's stand, the principal was lauding the deeds

of the graduating class in words grown dull with use through the years. Joseph grimaced imperceptibly and turned to steal a glance at Valerie. Her gaze was fixed attentively on the principal, but she caught his glance, and the corners of her mouth twitched upwards for the barest of instants. It was a beautiful mouth, Joseph thought. It told everything about her, her . . . breeding. It wasn't slack and loose like so many others he had seen. A fringe of black, solitary hairs wouldn't appear on her upper lip when she was old, like his . . . He stopped himself. He hadn't meant to do it. The thought had just slipped in. He had almost thought of his mother.

The white graduation cap coned to a point on her forehead, parting the burnished fairness of her hair like a silver cleft. There were soft hollows that planed down from high cheekbones, and her eyes were a startling brown, deep brown, almost black. For an instant, he could not understand how it had all come about, this thing that was between them. It had been only two weeks ago, that day when he had been looking at her in class, and she had turned and seen the adoration in his eyes. Even then he had been dimly aware that she was immensely flattered, and it was then that she first began speaking to him.

It was not that they had gone out together, or would ever go out. That was impossible. She was Richard Morris's girl and everyone knew it. Joseph understood that, but somehow it was almost as though she were his. Perhaps it didn't seem like much, but to Joseph it was a great deal.

A brittle burst of mechanical clapping suddenly filled the auditorium and Joseph noticed that the principal had given way to the superintendent of the school district. As the clapping diminished and died, he heard Valerie's whisper.

"Can you see your parents? I just found mine."

Though he purposely had not looked, he shook his head and muttered a barely audible, "Not yet. I don't know if they came."

Joseph tried then to keep his attention riveted on the figure of the superintendent. He was a tall man and he had been in the first war. People said that was why he always stood and walked as though he were marching, with his shoulders thrown back, his stomach pulled in, and his head erect. Joseph tried to listen, but again, the words from the speaker's stand faded into a flow of meaningless sounds.

He lowered his eyes and tried not to look for them in the rows of upturned faces. But something seemed to be pulling his eyes to the audience. Unaware that he was doing so, he glanced quickly at the reserved section, holding his breath, half expecting them to be sitting in the very front row. His eyes swept the length of the row and his breath sighed relievedly from his lungs. At least they were not there, not in the front row.

He stared at the floor for a time, then he glanced again toward the faces, his eyes darting wildly over the reserved section. He saw them. They were shockingly easy to find. They seemed to stand out like black against a wall of white. He stared at the floor, determined not to look again now that he had found them. But he was forced to look. He had to know if they really were that conspicuous in the wall of white.

They were in the middle of the fifth row, and even from the stage, Joseph could mark the million lines that seamed the face of his father, the thin shoulders and the sunken chest, garbed in the shining, worn black of the old wedding suit, the shirt buttoned at the throat, the tie with the bulky knot that forced the shirt flaps askew. His hair was iron gray, parted on the side and combed back. Joseph shuddered when he remembered what might have happened.

His father had taken the can of olive oil into the bathroom and had already poured a pool into the palm of one hand, ready to plaster it on his hair. Joseph had stepped into the bathroom to brush his teeth, and he had seen the olive oil.

"Pa!" he had gasped.

His father had stopped and lowered his hand.

"Wotsa matter?" he had asked in surprise, his eyes starting from his thin face.

Joseph had been furious. He had almost said something terrible about the olive oil. But instead, he had forced a smile and said in excitement, "Long as you're dressing up, you gotta try my hair oil for once. It's really good stuff."

His father had looked at him in silence, and for the second time that evening, Joseph had imagined he saw understanding in his father's eyes. But the old man had smiled quickly, and Joseph could not be certain.

"Shura, Joe. Tat's ver' nice-a you." And he had poured the olive oil back into the can from his leathered and veined hand.

Joseph could see the broad face of his mother, rimmed with coarse, graying hair, hair that was pulled back and bound in a knot behind her head. She was wearing the same black dress she wore to the little church every Sunday, the black dress that bound her close and showed the bulging fat above her hips and the rolls beneath her shoulder blades. And it was a ridiculous hat. It seemed to balance on her head like a pot with a lone, protruding flower. God, Joseph thought. They're so damned obvious. They're so damned old-country.

And as he watched them, a low wave of polite laughter spilled through the auditorium. The superintendent had said something funny. And Joseph watched as his father and mother looked about quickly and saw the laughing faces and knew that the speaker had made a joke, then smiled and laughed themselves, but too late, too late. Joseph lowered his head and closed his eyes in hopelessness, hopelessness mingled with a momentary surge of love for them and a guilty anger that he was feeling what he was.

It had been the same at the house that evening, before the graduation, when his mother had been ironing his white shirt. She had stopped suddenly and put her hand to her heart, and Joseph had seen it. It was a familiar gesture when she was tired.

"You're tired," he had said.

She had turned quickly and seen that he had been watching her, and she had smiled and resumed her ironing, too quickly.

"No, Joe. I'm all right."

But he had pressed the issue, at first feeling guilt at what he was doing, and then making himself almost believe that he was doing the right thing, for her.

"You better stay home, Ma. This affair's gonna be a long one. You might get sick."

A startled fear had leaped into her eyes, as though she were to be cheated of something very precious. She shook her head and said near frantically, "No, Joe. I'm all right. I'm wanta go, Joe. You my only boy, an' I gotta go."

Joseph hadn't insisted then. He had been flooded with a terrible tenderness for her. He had put his arm around her shoulders and kissed her forehead. "Okay, Ma," he had said and started towards his room. His father had been standing in the doorway, and Joseph imagined for an instant that his father knew what had transpired in his mind.

But the old man had looked at him and said, and his voice was almost soft, "Mama be okay, Joe. Don't worry."

On the speakers' platform, the superintendent had given way to the class valedictorian, and a burst of appreciative applause greeted the youth's impressive appearance. Looking at him, Joseph felt for the first time a deep and bitter resentment. Richard Morris was tall, with the shoulders and limber movements of an athlete. His blue gown hung gracefully and easily on him, and the blue cap did not completely hide the short, brushed curls that crept out from the cone of blue. He spoke easily and confidently.

Joseph wished that he himself were an athlete, that his grades were the highest in the class, or even that he could be good-looking. Perhaps then, he could have something to lean on. Perhaps then, he would not have to feel ashamed of anything. He could bet that Richard Morris would never have to feel shame for his parents, even if they happened to be old-country. He had too much to fall back on. Joseph lowered his eyes from the speaker's stand and tried to stare at the floor and not hear. Beside him, he could feel Valerie's occasional quiver of pride, and the resentment deepened until it died, and he felt nothing but a helpless emptiness.

There was a loud roar of applause from the audience when Richard Morris ended his speech. As usual, Joseph thought, he had done the right thing. He always did the right thing. His speech was short and pleasing, especially short, a thing for which the audience was unconsciously grateful.

As the ceremony ended, Joseph listened to the calling of the names and watched with mounting excitement as the students marched to the stand, took their diplomas, shook the superintendent's hand, and returned to their seats. When his own name was called, he set his face in a rigid mask and walked woodenly to the stand. There was a naked sensation of being alone, the feel of harsh, rolled paper in his left hand, the sweatiness of a palm against his, and then he was miraculously back in his own seat, feeling an immense relief to be back and buried in the midst of the graduates.

When the band again struck up the march and the graduates filed through the wings and down the aisle to the doors at the rear of the room, Joseph moved in limp exhaustion. It was all over, all over. It was not until then that he remembered.

When the line of blue and white passed through the rear doors, the graduates suddenly broke ranks and began filing back into the auditorium through the other door to greet their parents and friends.

Joseph was stunned. This was something he had not counted on. He wavered among the graduates uncertainly, and then permitted himself to be swept along by the unceremonious rush back into the auditorium. As he passed through the doors, he glimpsed his father's black coat in the other aisle. He started toward the coat, and then halted. His mind was reeling and he was confused. This was something he had not prepared for. He did not know what to do. He stood stock-still for a long moment, and then weaved through the laughter and the noise and the embraces to the side of the auditorium that was farthest from his parents.

He stood still again among the milling groups, torn between desire and a stricken reluctance. Craning his neck back and forth, he peered for another glimpse of them. Then he saw them. They were standing quietly against the far side of the auditorium. His father was regarding the embracing people with a confused smile, but his mother was glancing about searchingly. A pang that was heavy with guilt wracked Joseph through, and he started to make his way toward them. But it was then that he saw something that made him stop in his tracks. Directly beside the place where his mother and father waited, Valerie was standing with her parents.

Her face was radiant with happiness and she was babbling excitedly, but this was not what Joseph saw. He saw her mother, a slender woman dressed in something white and soft, and her father, a tall man with a graying, groomed head, about whose frame hung a tailored spring suit. Joseph waited in agony for them to move away, but as he waited, another group suddenly joined them in conversation. Joseph cast one helpless glance at his parents, and then turned away.

He never knew that at that moment, his father saw him and excitedly nudged the mother. She turned in time to see Joseph disappear among the mingling forms.

Joseph walked toward the door, almost sobbing in his helplessness. Directly before him in the whirling room, he saw Richard Morris introducing another graduate to his parents. Joseph saw two things, that his parents were, as he expected, fashionably dressed, and second, that the introduction was casually made. Joseph suddenly felt a raging hatred for all the people in the world who could introduce their parents with such casual confidence.

He was on the point of shouldering past the group when Richard Morris caught him by the shoulder. Before Joseph knew what had happened, he was being introduced to the youth's parents. He mumbled an incoherent hello, and then, in a daze, he heard Richard Morris's invitation.

"We're having a little party at my folks' place. Why don't you come along?"

Joseph's resentment faded into nothing and he was suffused with a sudden gratefulness. He smiled warmly at Richard and allowed himself to be guided out of the auditorium and into the night.

The street was lined with elms that stretched upwards toward the night sky. The street was silent, so that the sound of their footsteps fell hollow upon their ears. The mother walked with difficulty. She was tired, but she did not place her hand upon her heart. In the silence of the darkened street, there was the sound of a stifled sob, soft in the night.

The father had been walking with his eyes downcast. He raised his head now and placed an arm about the mother's shoulders. They walked into the shadow of the elms and were gone in the night.

# GUEST

## OF

## HONOR

The warden refrained from taking even the slightest of jig-steps. Still, as he walked down the last steel corridor that led to death row, there was an unmistakable airiness in the hollow echo of his footsteps.

He was a florid man with the prosperous padding of a political appointee in good times. He had not yet removed his hat since returning from town, and locks of his long and snowy mane peeked from beneath the brim in back. His neck was shaved clean and his moustache was trimmed, and he gave off a barbershop aroma of spices and lotions.

The guard at the entrance to death row had seen him approaching, and the steel-barred door was open when he arrived. The warden noticed that he was in need of a shave and almost mentioned it to him. Then he remembered that this guard would not be taking Staug to the gas chamber in the morning.

But the next guard, the one at the control desk before the death row cells, would be, and the warden saw with increasing irritation that he too had a stubble and that his uniform was wrinkled and spattered in front with grease spots.

"Haven't you got a cleaner uniform than that?" he asked.

Jensen, the death row guard, looked down at his uniform as if seeing it for the first time. "Yeah, warden," he said, blinking slowly from a fleshy face. "I think so."

"Well, get it on before tomorrow morning," the warden said. "The governor's going to be here, you know."

"I didn't know," Jensen said.

There was a long barred enclosure with tables separating the control desk and the death row cells, and the warden peered through the bars toward Staug's steel cubicle.

"You wanta go into his cell?" Jensen said, reaching for a lever.

"No, you damned fool," the warden muttered in a low voice. "D'you think I want to get next to that maniac?" And in a louder voice, he added, "Let me into the enclosure, Jensen."

The door slid open and the warden crossed the enclosure toward the cell. He was near enough by now so that his barbershop scents wafted to the death row prisoners. There was a moan of ecstasy from one of them. "Oh, Monty!" he said to the warden. "Your perfume is lovely."

The warden almost grinned self-consciously, and then sniffed in disdain. He stopped before Staug's cell, but stayed a reasonable distance from the bars. Staug was lying on his cot, looking at the ceiling.

"Staug," the warden called.

"Yeah," said Staug without raising his head.

"I'm sorry," the warden intoned solemnly. "But I've got bad news for you. The commutations board denied your appeal for mercy. There'll be no life sentence."

"Yeah, I know," said Staug. "I heard it over the radio."

The warden was flustered. "I'm sorry," he said, repeating himself.

Staug swung his legs over the side of the cot. "I'll bet you are," he said.

The warden cleared his throat uncomfortably. "I'll send the chaplain up again if you promise to be good to him."

When Staug didn't answer, the warden said, "Well, is there anything you want then? You're entitled to one last request, you know."

"How about a gas mask?" said Staug. There was a guffaw from one of the other cells. Staug stood up and came over to the cell door. The warden instinctively shuffled back a few inches.

"You can have a nice steak dinner if you want," the warden said mildly.

Staug shrugged. "What difference does it make?" In the naked light of death row, his eyes showed the dangerous glitter of a mind off kilter.

There was an uneasy silence as Staug's gaze flickered to the warden's trimmed moustache and haircut. "All duded up, huh?"

The warden grinned embarrassedly. "Well, I was in town anyway, you know," he began to explain, and then stopped. "The governor's going to be here in the morning," he said. "It's the first time he's ever come, you know."

"Well, that just makes the party, doesn't it?" Staug mocked. Then the smile disappeared. "So how's that supposed to make me feel?"

The warden had had enough. "Well, Staug," he said. "I'd like to say goodbye. It's been good knowing you."

Staug threw back his head and laughed wildly. "Oh, for cripe's sake!" he gasped, and sank on the cot in laughter.

The warden's neck was still flushed as he took his leave of death row. He wondered why he had ever gone up in the first place, except perhaps that he thought Staug should know the governor was going to be there. *And he wasn't even impressed,* the warden thought bitterly.

He shook his head. Sometimes, he just couldn't understand their attitude up there. Always making trouble of some sort. Like the time after dinner when Staug had managed to burst through the door to the enclosure before the guard could shut it. Of course it had been a foolish attempt, but he had managed to cut up the guard with a knife he'd gotten from God knows where.

And then there was the time, again during dinner, when two of them had sliced each other with razor blades. The warden remembered he had had quite some difficulty explaining both incidents to the governor, but had finally half-convinced him that knives and razors were always showing up in prison, no matter how much precaution you took. Still, the warden could get some satisfaction in that all this had made for one of the most publicized executions in the history of the prison.

Before going to his office, the warden took another quick inspection tour of the waiting room where the governor and the press would assemble. "I want this room dusted again the last thing tonight," he told the front desk clerk. "And Clyde, don't forget to make sure everybody's got on clean uniforms and white shirts." He paused before going into his office and added, "Remember, nobody gets in that front door without an invitation."

In his office, he called up the newspapers and told them gravely that Staug had said he was prepared to pay for his terrible crimes and that he was resigned to his fate. As his last wish, he was having a full-course steak dinner, and then would spend his last hours in prayer with the chaplain. And, he added, had they heard that the governor was going to be there?

When his duties were done, he crossed the outer yard to his house, a stone building that was a little grim on the outside, but elaborate and richly furnished on the inside. It was one of the better compensations of the job.

Throughout dinner, his wife, Emmy, spoke only a few words. It was obvious that she was more apprehensive than usual. But she did not mention it until the houseboy, a prison trustee, had cleared away the table and gone into the kitchen. "Monty," she said, "I can understand a nice breakfast for the governor, but I'm wondering about the flowers. It just doesn't seem right, somehow."

"What're you talking about?" the warden flared. "This is an

occasion. How many times do you think I get a chance to have the governor here?"

And that ended that. They spoke no more through the dessert, and afterwards, the warden retired early so that he would be refreshed in the morning. Before going to bed, he phoned one last time to death row. "He's sound asleep, warden," Jensen answered breezily. "All curled up in his blankets and sleeping like a rock."

The sky was still black when the warden arose in the morning. He had slept but little that night, and he was irritated, but the shower restored him. He shaved and dressed carefully in the dark blue suit, taking a long time before the mirror in his bedroom. By the time he finished his coffee and toast, he was behind schedule. Still, he took one last turn in front of the mirror before scurrying out the door and across the yard to the prison.

A number of guests had already arrived, but the warden saw with a huge sigh of relief that the governor was not yet there. He bustled into the waiting room and shook hands warmly with everyone, ignoring the knowing, reluctant response of some of the newspapermen. When he finally realized that the phone in his office had been ringing for some time, he was in a state of high excitement. Excusing himself, he walked quickly into his office to pick up the phone. A thought crossed his mind, and he held his breath against the possibility that the governor had changed his mind and would not be there.

Jensen, the death row guard, had to repeat himself three times before it registered on the warden. "I don't know how it happened," the voice wheezed over the phone in frenzy. "He got ahold of a razor blade somewhere. All the time, I thought he was sleeping like a rock, but he was dead."

The warden could not hang up the phone. It slipped from his fingers to the desk with a clatter and lay there. Jensen's voice could still be heard, squawking without meaning through the receiver. The warden sank back in his padded chair and stared frozenly before him. He was still in that position when Clyde, the front desk clerk, burst into the office with the announcement, "The governor is here!"

# NIGHT

## RIDE

*. . . From the manner in which Guzzi was slain, Chicago police believe that his death can be laid at gangland's doors. He was cut down by shotgun blasts while entering his garage tonight. Police reported there were no immediate clues as to the identity of the assailants.*

Lido Scarpelli reached forward and switched off the radio. His square, bulging body settled comfortably back into the yielding depth of the seat cushions, and an expression of satisfaction came over his fleshy face. The headlight beams poked long fingers of white into the darkness of the Nevada desert.

Twenty-five thousand through the nose, he mused. A lot of money, but it was worth every buck. He had to hand it to the boys. Their price was hell-high, but they always did a neat job. He shook his head and felt a brief wonder at how neat it really was. *No immediate clues.* Scarpelli chuckled aloud. That was a laugh. *No damned clues at all* was what the announcer should have said. He chuckled again as he imagined how that would have sounded over the radio. Then, glancing swiftly out the side window, he grimaced at the blackness. God, not a light for miles. How the hell did the yokels stand it?

He squirmed uncomfortably. He didn't like the feeling of being so completely alone. But Las Vegas wasn't too far away. Maybe a dozen miles. And it was necessary as hell. Picturing the confusion in Chicago, he smiled in private pleasure. Guzzi's wife would be shouting that Scarpelli was behind the shooting. And the coppers would no doubt have visited his home by now.

Why, no, officers. Lido's not here. He left three days ago for Las Vegas. Business, you know. He's driving. Should be there by now. Yes, he'll be staying at the Mesquite Hotel.

Scarpelli could picture Mae saying it. Good girl, Mae. And the coppers would check, and what d'you know? Scarpelli really is at the Mesquite. Neat as hell. Scarpelli clucked his tongue in amusement and the satisfied expression deepened.

Releasing one hand from the steering wheel, he shoved back the snap-brim fedora and dug his fingers into his thinning black hair. He scratched the itch thoughtfully for a moment, then replaced the hat and leaned forward, his narrow, black eyes squinting into the darkness. It was a moment before he realized what it was. The figure of a man was outlined dimly in the far reaches of the headlights. He was thumbing.

But as the car neared the figure, Scarpelli saw that he didn't look very clean. Old leather jacket and such. Not on these seat cushions, he thought. He passed the figure, and again, only the blackness of the desert night loomed before him.

Then he felt a sudden twinge of sympathy. God, all alone in this forsaken country. Scarpelli decided he could afford to be expansive. He pressed his foot down on the brake, and when the car finally came to a stop, he eased it into reverse and backed up. The hitchhiker met him halfway.

When he opened the door, Scarpelli saw in the brief flare of light that he was only a kid. Twenty years old if he was lucky. He was dressed in an old leather jacket, black and worn through at one elbow, and corduroy trousers. His hair was uncombed, sort of a dirty brown and long, and there was an uncertain fuzz of moustache on his upper lip. He sank down into the cushions awkwardly.

"Thanks, mister. I was beginnin' to think no one would ever come by."

He's probably never been in a boat like this, thought Scarpelli. "Forget it, kid," he said. "What're you doing way out here?" The car moved forward with a powerful, muted roar.

The kid gestured over his shoulder with his thumb. "Farmer dumped me off back a ways. I been walkin' fer hours." He was regarding Scarpelli in the half light from the broad dashboard.

Scarpelli felt suddenly important. Probably never seen clothes like this either, he thought, unconsciously flicking an imaginary speck of dust from his pin-striped knee. He fished into his side pocket and produced a studded cigarette case. Pressing the button, he held it in front of the kid. "Smoke?"

"Yeah, thanks," the kid answered, grubbing into the glittering case for a cigarette.

When he had one, Scarpelli took his own from the farthest end, where the dirty fingers hadn't touched. He'd have to empty the case and put some clean cigarettes in, he thought, after he'd dumped the kid.

The kid produced his own match and lit his cigarette, then reached over to light Scarpelli's. In the flare of light, Scarpelli saw that his face was gaunt. Maybe he's more than twenty, he thought.

The kid smoked in silence, his eyes straight ahead to the highway. Scarpelli wished he would say something.

"Where you headed?" he asked.

"Vegas," the kid answered, and drew deep on his cigarette.

Scarpelli watched as the burn rim on the kid's cigarette smouldered hot. "Me too," he said, and looked away. "I'll take you all the way in."

There was a shower of sparks from the side of the car. When Scarpelli glanced around, he saw that the kid had spread his legs and was brushing frantically at the seat.

"Better stop, mister," he said. "I dropped my smoke on the seat." He paused, then added, "I'm sorry as hell, mister."

Scarpelli pressed his foot down firmly on the brake, his heavy brows knit in irritation. Clumsy jerk, he thought. The car moved to a stop on the side of the road and Scarpelli turned in his seat.

But the kid wasn't fishing for the cigarette. He was braced against the door, and there was a gun in his hand. In the light from the dashboard, his face was tight. He was breathing rapidly.

"Okay, mister. Hand it over," he said in an unsteady voice.

For a long moment, Scarpelli could not seem to comprehend what the kid had said. He regarded him with open-mouthed stupefaction, his eyes traveling dumbly from the thin, blue barrel of the pistol to the white, strained face. He had a sudden, incongruous realization that the pistol, for God's sake, was a .22.

"Huh?" he grunted.

"Money. Gimme your money," the kid ordered, and this time, there was an edge of frenzy in his voice.

A sickly grin crossed Scarpelli's face, then vanished. He did not even know he had complied with the order. Groping in his pocket for the wallet, he held it forward. The kid snatched it quickly, opened it with one hand, his eyes still watching Scarpelli, fingered the roll of bills, and then stuffed the wallet into his jacket pocket. The money seemed to give him confidence.

Scarpelli finally found his voice. "Kid! For God's sake, kid!" he pleaded in a stricken voice. "You can't do this to me! I'm Lido Scarpelli!"

"Who?"

"Scarpelli! Lido Scarpelli!"

"So what?" the kid asked guardedly.

"Don't you know who I am? Don't you read the papers?"

"I only read the funnies," the kid said sincerely, but with a trace of irritation, as though he were anxious to be about something.

Scarpelli made one last effort. "I'm with the mobs, kid! I'm with the mobs! Chicago!" he croaked.

The kid's lips twisted in a grin. "Yeah?" he murmured, but still, he leaned forward and moved one long hand rapidly over the pinstripe suit. He found only the cigarette case, which he pocketed.

"Where's your gun?"

For an instant, Scarpelli was struck dumb. "Gun?" he echoed. "Gun? We don't carry guns no more. That was in the old days."

The kid grinned wider, and then, his face set suddenly in tight lines. "Get out," he ordered. "Get outa the car."

Scarpelli stared at him blankly for a moment. Then, he moved one hand mechanically to the door and opened it. But as he was stepping out, a sudden thought seemed to paralyze him. He turned slowly, the incredulity gone from his face. The kid had moved to the driver's seat and was stepping out of the car.

Scarpelli lurched backwards, his hands raised before him, the palms toward the kid. "No, no," he croaked. "Don't do it, kid! For God's sake, don't do it! I got a family! Think of my family!"

The kid regarded him puzzledly. "Don't do what . . ." Then, comprehending for the first time, he muttered in surprise, "I'm not goin' to kill ya. Just stand clear of the car, that's all."

Scarpelli stumbled backwards a few more steps, and the kid stepped swiftly into the driver's seat.

"But . . . but . . . ," Scarpelli croaked.

The kid closed the door and lowered the window. "Well, thanks mister. Darned nice of you," he grinned, then added in afterthought, "See you in Chicago sometime."

Scarpelli watched as the car rumbled forward on the highway, watched as the half-moon of white from the headlights grew smaller in the distance. A crimson flush mounted over his starched white collar and suffused his fleshy face.

Clenching his fist, he shook it at the retreating car. "The coppers! I'll tell the coppers!" he roared, then winced as he suddenly pictured what the coppers would say, what the newspapers would say. He could never tell them. Never.

The half-moon of white disappeared over a faraway rise, and for the first time, Scarpelli noticed the blackness about him. A coyote yipped in the far distance, and Scarpelli started at the sound. Then, glancing apprehensively at the desert, he plunged his hands in his pockets and started walking.

# CROSSROADERS

The young man with the black hair glanced again at the two cards in his hand. Through the cone of light that flooded the felt-covered twenty-one table, he gazed absently at the expressionless face of the dealer.

"Hit," he murmured, and watched as the dealer flipped over the card. It was a face card, a queen.

"Bust," the young man said indifferently, facing the cards in his hand. He straightened on his stool and watched as the dealer dealt himself a card. It was a six. He laid it deftly on the ten and four.

"Twenty," he muttered dryly.

To the left of the young man, the player with the scorched, bloated face slapped his cards down on the felt. A deep flush purpled the heavy flesh that hung below his eyes. "Nineteen," he said thickly, angrily. "Christ, what luck."

To the right of the young man, the girl with the strangely oblique, gray eyes turned her cards over slowly. "Twenty," she said, her voice empty of emotion. "Push."

The dealer scooped up the cards with quick, practiced movements. The diamonds set flush into the band on his finger glittered in the cone of light.

The young man rose from the stool and twisted his shoulders in a half stretch. He was tall and lean, and there were hollows beneath the cheekbones that ridged his face. In a tiny arc across the bridge of his nose, there was a thin, new scar.

"That's enough for me tonight, DeNello," he said to the dealer. "See you tomorrow."

DeNello nodded, his blue eyes lighting suddenly as he grinned a quick, tight grin. He looked down and shuffled the cards in a rhythmic fluttering. The young man turned to the girl.

"Come on, Pat. I'll buy you a drink."

The girl looked questioningly at the dealer. But the player with the bloated face spoke up. "I don't like to play alone," he said, his voice heavy with irritation.

Pat shrugged. She looked at the young man. "I guess I stay, Paul. Maybe next time."

Paul nodded and turned away from the table. At the bar, he leaned easily against the polished railing and lighted a cigarette. The bartender's hulking shoulders loomed before him.

"What'll it be, Mr. Collier?" he asked hoarsely.

Paul surveyed the massive face. "Scotch and water, Danny," he said. When the bartender had returned, he asked, "What's all the noise down there?"

Danny laughed throatily. "Some cowpoke giving a dude a rough time."

Paul listened idly as the cowhand's slow Texan drawl carried to his ears and then leaned back to look at the group.

The cowhand was perched easily on the edge of his stool, his long legs stretched out to the floor, his sweat-stained hat set back on his head. He wore a clean, faded jumper and his Levi's were creased and dirty from long wear. His angular, tanned face was wreathed in smiles as he ribbed the dude, who had turned his back on the man and was frantically striving to carry on a conversation with an embarrassed brunette.

The cowhand surveyed the back of the silk cowboy shirt and the spotless riding pants. "Why, ah bet you ain't nevah been on a hoss," he drawled.

Paul gulped down his drink. "And ah bet you ain't nevah been to Texas, cowboy," he murmured to himself as he left the bar and walked into the night.

Moving casually down the long line of cars parked before the club, he stopped at a green coupe and climbed in. Two men in a black sedan sat motionless, watching him.

Paul backed away from the curb and swung onto the main highway leading into Reno. Behind him, the black sedan waited until the coupe had disappeared from sight, and then pulled away from the club.

In the darkness of the parking lot behind his hotel, Paul's car came to a stop. Climbing out, he weaved swiftly through the maze of parked cars and eased into the side entrance to the lobby. In the elevator, the short man standing before him removed his hat from a bald head, glanced about embarrassedly, and then put it on again in the strained silence.

Inside his room, Paul jerked his coat off roughly and heaved it onto the bed. He walked to the dresser and pulled open the top drawer. It was then that a knock sounded at the door.

Pushing the drawer shut, Paul walked to the door and turned the key. The two men brushed past him into the room.

The one with the thin face and blade-like nose spoke first. "What the hell's up, Paul? Why no signal?"

Paul raised his hands in a gesture of helplessness. "I couldn't cut him, Wade. I'll be damned if I could."

The third man sat down carefully on the bed, pulling up the slack in his trousers to preserve the crease. He wore a neatly trimmed moustache. "He's flat though, isn't he?" he asked.

"Flatter than hell. When I left, he was really cleaning a live one."

"Did you give those cards the works?" demanded Wade.

"I checked them out for everything," Paul answered perplexedly. "They're clean as a whistle. I can't figure it out."

"Are you sure you gave them everything, Paul?" the man on the bed asked.

Paul turned to him. "Everything, Pete," he said bitterly. "I ran the whole gamut. The cards weren't crimped, they lay flat to the table. The edges were clear, not a sign of a shave. I tried everything, pinpricks, daubs, even sorts. Not a damned thing. I don't know what the hell to think."

The man named Pete rose from the bed. "Where's your whiskey, Paul? I'll mix us a drink. That was a long wait in the car."

"In the top drawer. Glasses in the bathroom," Paul answered. He flopped into an armchair. "I don't wonder Cliff couldn't crack him."

Wade eased a chair away from the desk and sat down. "Is he getting wise to you?"

"No. Tonight, he second-carded us to death without batting an eye. Before, he's pulled in his horns every once in a while."

Wade unbuttoned his coat. The black butt of the pistol in his shoulder holster came into view. He stretched his legs out, resting them on their heels. "Is he working through a shill?" he asked.

Paul flushed suddenly. "There's a girl at the table, but she's square."

Pete emerged from the bathroom, a drink in each hand. "You mean a shill?" he asked puzzledly.

"I mean a *girl*."

Wade interrupted quickly. "Where does she play, Paul?"

Paul's features relaxed. "She never plays to his right," he answered.

Wade fell silent, shaking his head slowly. "I don't know. I don't know," he said. "We can't waste our whole lives on one lousy joint."

"What does the chief say?" asked Paul.

"He wants the goods on DeNello. He's not going to like this," answered Wade ruefully.

"Do you want to close up the game and bluff it out on my word that he's a digger?" asked Paul.

"It won't hold up in court," Wade answered bitterly. "We tried that when Cliff couldn't find anything. We went over that deck with a microscope, but it was clean. Hell, DeNello's lawyer had the game open the next day, and there wasn't a damned thing we could do about it."

Paul set his drink down on the end table and fumbled for a cigarette. "Well, what'll we do then?"

Wade rose to his feet and buttoned his coat. "Give it another try. He's doing something, we know that. All we have to do is find out what," he said wryly. "We'll be outside same time tonight."

They paused at the door as Paul asked, "How're the other boys doing?"

"Good," answered Wade. "They finished with the big clubs tonight. Not a sharper in the bunch. I don't know why we even bother with them."

Pete spoke up, amusement wrinkling his eyes. "Tommy ran into something funny," he said. "He's checking out this little joint, you know, where the dealer has been clean all night. Tommy gets set to go, when up comes this southerner, loaded and loud. He planks a stack of bills on the table and says, 'Ah've got a thousand dollars heah and ah'm goin' to gamble. Ah knows mah cahd-shahpin', brothah, and if ah catch you second-cahding me, ah'll break yore neck.'"

Paul laughed aloud at Pete's imitation of the southerner.

"Well, anyway," Pete continued. "Tommy says the dealer's lips get all thin and he reaches way down for a new deck. They start playing, and inside of a half hour, that dealer had second-carded the southerner out of most of that roll. Tommy walks out about then and gives us the signal. We walk in, grab the deck, and close up the game. The southerner was fit to be tied."

"What about the dealer?" Paul asked.

"Well, he really felt bad," answered Pete. "He says he's been a square John for years, and then this character had to come in and say something like that."

Paul chuckled as Wade and Pete pulled the door shut behind

them. Gamblers were a strange lot, he mused, remembering the old man in the boardinghouse at Elko, the old man who had taught him the tricks of the sharper. "Never let the sucker go un-plucked," he had said. "If he can't see what's happening to him, he'll never know. And if he never knows, he'll never be hurt."

Paul remembered how the words had come back to him in Las Vegas, when he had been forced to show himself before Lou Cro-setti could hide his crooked deck. Crosetti had been like an ani-mal in his rage. They had tried to lecture to him, but the words had slid off Crosetti's back like water. "It's un-American!" he had shouted over and over in his outraged indignation. He could not be told he was doing wrong.

Paul wondered if DeNello lived by the same code. Certainly, the man was at least aware of the law, to conceal his way of cheat-ing so completely. But he probably considered it only as a safe-guard against the necessary evil of the gambling commission, and let it go at that.

DeNello was a funny customer, Paul mused. Away from the ta-ble, he spoke freely and was constantly aware of his appearance. He held his chin high to hide the roll of flesh that threatened a double chin. His stomach was sucked in, his carriage erect.

And yet, behind the table, he seemed to become oblivious to himself. Paul remembered how his jaw became slack and the double chin became a reality, how his stomach protruded, and how he suddenly became untalkative. He would speak no more than a dozen words during hours behind the table. It was a weird, silent game when DeNello dealt. About the only attraction at the table was Pat.

Paul winced as he remembered. He wondered what Wade and Pete thought of his insistence that she was a girl, not a shill. And he wondered why, for the first time, he should make the distinc-tion. It was then he realized that she did not belong to a table. Her softly contoured features, her bearing, and above all, her soft-spoken graciousness stood out in shocking contrast to the usual, the painted, weary, rasping shill.

And where had DeNello picked her up? Associating the two names disturbed him strangely. DeNello fitted with the painted shills. Pat didn't belong. Suddenly, Paul found himself glad that there was to be another night at the club.

He tried to concentrate on DeNello. As Wade had said, he was doing something. Paul tried to piece together the pattern of the game. It was a cinch DeNello wasn't the best of second-card dealers. There were times he lost good hands even when he sharped a card. It seemed as though he were just boosting the odds a little in his favor.

Boosting the odds a little. Boosting the odds a little. Paul's brows furrowed as something in the far reaches of his mind begged to be heard. Boosting the odds. The words had a connection somewhere.

Slowly at first and then in a sudden flood, he remembered. The old-timer from Elko had said it. "The cheater who will never be caught is the sequence dealer, the one in a million, the one who doesn't need a marked deck or a shiner, the one who remembers the cards in the order in which he picks them up, the one who boosts the odds a little."

The cigarette scorched Paul's fingers and he snuffed it out quickly in the ashtray. That was it. DeNello was the one in a million, the sequence dealer. He was the cheater with the mathematical mind, the perfect memory. All the pieces fit together—the orderly way in which he picked up the discards, the meticulous shuffling, and the silence, the silence in which DeNello concentrated on the position of the high cards.

But with the sudden exultation of his discovery came the knowledge that there was still nothing the gambling commission could do. There was no marked deck, no concrete evidence. DeNello was in the clear.

Paul groaned aloud as he rose and shed his clothes for bed. He could be wrong about the sequence. He hoped he was wrong. He hoped bitterly that he was.

It was a Monday night, a quiet early-week night, and DeNello's was caught in the awkward lull that follows a weekend of loud voices and loud laughter. There was an occasional, muted murmur from the handful of persons at the bar, and the music box played a soft, unintelligible melody. At the gambling table, Paul slouched casually on his stool and made ready to try his experiment. DeNello had just finished shuffling. He was beginning his deal.

"How long you been here, DeNello?" Paul asked.

DeNello stopped short in his deal and stared at Paul, an expression of complete surprise on his face.

"Huh?" he grunted.

Paul picked up his first card, glanced at it, and set it down. "I said how long you been in Reno?"

"About two years," DeNello answered perplexedly. "Why?"

"Nothing," Paul answered. "Just curious." He waited until DeNello had resumed his deal. Then he asked, "You from the West originally?"

DeNello stopped again, his eyes hot with irritation. "No, from Detroit," he said in a controlled voice, looking hard at Paul, and then at the other players, who were glancing at him impatiently.

Paul stole quick glances at DeNello's hands as he resumed dealing. His stomach tightened when DeNello started to slip out a second card, faltered for the briefest of instants, then shoved it back into the deck. He dealt out the hand without a single second card. Paul concentrated on his own hand. He could feel DeNello's eyes on him through the cone of light.

An hour later, Paul looked at his wristwatch. It was one o'clock. He straightened and eased down from the stool. "I might as well move my bed down here, DeNello," he grinned. "I'll see you tonight."

DeNello nodded and began to shuffle the deck. Paul turned to the girl. "Come on, Pat. There's three on the table. Let's have a drink."

Pat did not bother to look at DeNello this time. She flashed Paul a quick, grateful smile and fell in beside him. DeNello's eyes followed their retreating figures.

At the bar, she leaned forward to catch the flame from Paul's match. He felt a sudden, unaccountable hurt as her hand brushed his and was thankful when the cigarette was lit, when her nearness was gone.

She sat erect on the stool and faced him. "Where are you from, Paul?" she asked.

"Southern California. Long Beach," he lied.

"Here for the cure?"

For a reason that he could not explain, Paul did not want to lie to the girl. He wanted suddenly and desperately to tell her that he was alone, that there never had been anyone. He looked down at his drink and nodded.

"I'm sorry I asked, Paul. You don't have to talk about it," she said. There was a genuine regret in her voice, mingled with the faintest trace of longing.

Paul raged inwardly. She had misinterpreted his silence. She probably thought he was still in love with a wife who didn't exist. Again he felt the overwhelming desire to tell her the truth.

"It's all right, Pat," he said instead. "I wasn't thinking about her. She's not worth thinking about. She's a bitch." And when he had said it, he could have bitten his tongue out.

"Don't talk like that," she was saying. "I really didn't want to hear that. It seems to be the fashion here to call one's husband a bastard, one's wife a bitch. I hate the words."

Paul knew the rebuke had brought an embarrassed flush to his face. He said hurriedly, forcing a smile, "Sorry, Pat. Forget it. Guess I'm too affected by what's supposed to be the thing to do. Can I take you home when you get off?" He asked the question quite without realizing what he had said.

Pat's expression became troubled. She turned to glance at the gambling table, and then at the bartender, bent over a drink at the end of the bar. She leaned close to Paul suddenly, and her nearness birthed again the strange hurt within him, a thickness in his throat. He hardly heard her words. "All right, Paul. But not here. I'll meet you somewhere."

Paul knew his voice sounded unnatural. "Okay, but why not here? What's up?"

"I can't tell you now. I'll explain later. Where do you want me to meet you?"

"There's a little club near the arch, the Piccadilly. I'll be waiting by the door," he answered hurriedly.

She nodded as Paul slid from the stool and smiled a good-bye. He walked from the club without a sideward glance toward Danny, standing behind the bar.

As he pulled away from the curb, he waited until the headlights of Wade's sedan were framed in the rear-view mirror, and then drove swiftly into Reno. The signal light at the crossroads was red. He waited impatiently for it to change, then turned to the left and stopped on a darkened side street. When the sedan had parked, he jumped into the back seat.

Wade spoke first, as Paul was clambering through the door. "What's the matter this time?"

Paul spoke rapidly of the suspicion that occurred to him after Wade and Pete had left his hotel room, of his experiment at the twenty-one table, and of DeNello's confusion.

Pete voiced the rub. "But where does that leave us? We're not much better off than before."

Paul grasped at the straw. He had not known how to explain his meeting with the girl, but now there was an explanation, even though he took no stock in it himself.

"I've got an angle. I'm going to meet the girl, the one at the table, in a few minutes. There's a chance DeNello may have confided in her. If he did, her testimony might hold. It's our only out."

Wade was skeptical. "I don't know, Paul. If she gets wise that you're an agent, we're cooked again."

"We're cooked anyway," Paul argued. "There's nothing to lose, even if she does figure me out."

Wade deliberated silently for a moment and then agreed reluctantly. "Okay. Give it a try," he said, and then muttered to himself, "Cripes, what a mess."

Paul waited until the sedan had disappeared, then grinned broadly at his deception. He swung the coupe towards downtown Reno.

He was standing near the door, drink in hand, when Pat came in. Taking her by the arm, he guided her through the gloom to a circular booth by the fireplace.

Paul waited until they had lighted cigarettes. Then he asked, "Why didn't you want me to wait around, Pat?"

She dropped her eyes to the cigarette in her hand as she spoke. "It's DeNello," she said hesitantly. "I guess he sort of considers me his girl."

Resentment stiffened in Paul like a ramrod. He strained to keep it out of his voice. "I didn't know."

Pat looked up. "You caught me off guard, Paul," she said. "It's such a strange situation. I don't love him or anything like that. It's sort of an obligation, I guess you'd call it."

"Meaning what?"

"Well, he was decent enough to give me a job when I was broke. I appreciate that."

"You don't look like the broke type," Paul said. "Can I ask what happened?"

"I don't mind," she said. "It's no ghastly secret. I had money when I came to Reno, but the gambling fever hit me. Something like it has you, I think. When I finally came up for air, all my money was gone, and most of it right over the table where I'm working now."

Paul clenched his teeth to keep from shouting out the words. Decent of DeNello to give her a job. Decent as hell, after sharping her out of her money.

Pat was speaking again. "You know a strange thing?" she said. "These weeks of working at that table have actually given me a hatred of gambling. Can you understand that?"

Paul nodded, relaxing with the change in conversation. He understood it more than she could realize, he thought. "Did you come here for a divorce?" he asked.

"Yes," she answered, and then paused. "And from a nice guy, one of the nicest ever."

"Are you sorry now?" Paul asked hesitantly, fearing her answer.

She regarded him thoughtfully for a moment, and then shook her head slowly. "No, I'm not sorry." There was a plea for understanding in her voice. "I wanted something more than the usual out of my marriage. It wasn't there."

She paused, and Paul asked quietly, "What makes for more than the usual?"

The plea came into her voice again. "I wanted a husband to love," she said. "A husband who loved me, and most important of all, a husband who wanted to be with me more than anyone else. It was selfish, I'll grant that. But it was a right selfishness." She looked down at her drink. "When a good time for him began to mean our going out with other couples, it was the beginning. And when I found myself looking for the same kind of escape, it was the end. But I could realize that, and I was selfish enough not to want that for my life." Her voice suddenly became bitter. "So I came to Reno. I reached the crossroads, looking back upon what was at least a bearable existence and looking ahead to old dreams reborn. Now, I'm stalled here, and the old dreams are getting a little faded around the edges with the prospect of some pretty shabby affairs. You tell me where it ends."

Paul reached across the table suddenly and clasped her hand. She looked up and smiled, a quick, self-conscious smile. "That's the gruesome tale, Paul. What's yours?"

Caught off guard, Paul hesitated momentarily, and then shrugged his shoulders. "It's not even interesting. Just a big mistake not worth talking about."

"That's not fair," she chided.

"It's fair enough," he said. "Come on, I'll take you home." He waited until she had finished her drink, then walked beside her to the door. When she stepped into the coupe, the thickness came again into his throat.

As they mounted the stairs to her apartment, she handed him the key. He took it silently, hating the thing that hurt within him. At the door, he turned the key in the lock and stepped back. She stood in the open doorway and turned hesitantly.

His eyes met hers, and the desire that was in his eyes was reflected in hers. He felt the tortured pause that he had felt before, the moment when desire and reluctance are held in abeyance until the word is given. But this time, he did not want to enter.

"Won't you come in?" She did not speak his name, for names were something that could not be spoken in moments like these.

He did not know he had spoken until the words fell on his ears, hoarsely. "I better not." Then he was walking away, his movements stiff, the skin of his face drawn tight. He knew he had shamed her.

He was at the first landing when he saw DeNello. The dealer's pallid face was set in hard lines. His lips were thin and colorless.

"What the hell you doing here?" The question was ominous, insulting.

Paul felt the muscles of his arms and back tense with the urge to smash his fists into the unprotected face. But the curb rose to fight down the emotion that flooded his body. He could not antagonize the man now. It would ruin everything.

The tension eased out of his arms and he stammered apologetically, "Sorry, DeNello. I didn't know she was your girl."

DeNello's voice was cold and sneering. "You know it now. Keep your hands off."

Then Paul did the thing which he knew would cause many nights of torture when he remembered it. He extended his hand to DeNello, steeling himself against the soft palm that met his.

"No hard feelings, DeNello." And when the man nodded, Paul said, "See you tomorrow night. We'll have a drink."

As Paul turned to pass down the stairs, he glanced swiftly at DeNello's retreating back. At the head of the stairs, her face mirrored with shame and a disbelieving contempt, stood Pat. Paul's eyes met her, and then he turned away, the sickness of what he had done flooding over him in waves of helpless rage and nausea.

And in the darkness of his room, as he lay on his bed, he felt for the first time a sensation of hopeless loss. He knew then that he was in love with the girl. Lifting the bottle to his lips, he gulped down the gagging, burning liquid. When it was empty, he fell back in a dreamless sleep.

Through the hours of the next afternoon, he lay on the bed and felt the chilling breezes from the Sierra wash over him. Late in the afternoon he called Wade and told him he would visit the club again that night.

As he entered the club and approached the bar, Paul saw the sly, knowing smile on Danny's lips and knew the bartender had heard of his humiliation. Paul ordered his drink, flipping the silver dollar onto the bar in a cheap, condescending gesture, enjoying the anger that flared in Danny's face. Then Paul turned and surveyed the club.

It was late, nearly midnight, and there were only a handful of customers at the bar. Paul's eyes swung to the twenty-one table, and he saw the girl. She was standing with her back to him, idly clinking the silver dollars before her. The overhead lamp reflected the tawny sleekness of her hair. Paul downed his drink and sauntered slowly to the table.

Avoiding Pat's eyes, he found a stool to the far left of the table. There were two players between him and the girl, and for this he was glad.

He placed a ten-dollar bill down beside the betting spot, nodded a greeting to DeNello, and received his ten silver dollars. DeNello did not return the greeting and Paul saw the furious hate in his eyes. He wondered briefly what had happened in the apartment after he had left.

Splitting the silver dollars into even piles, he placed two on the bet spot and waited for DeNello to deal. But the dealer's cold voice snapped Paul's head up quickly.

"The limit's off for you, Collier. Bet as high as you want."

Paul glanced swiftly at Pat. His glance caught her unawares, and he saw pride mingled with the shame in her eyes. Then he knew what had happened, and knew also that DeNello was striking back at him the only way he knew how. The man was out to break him.

Opening his wallet, Paul thumbed through the bills. Less than a hundred dollars. Not enough to last for very long, he thought. But there was no leaving. He would have to ride it out for a break.

A player with a bloated face spoke up from the other side of the table. "That go for the whole table?"

DeNello turned, his voice cold. "This game's closed for tonight. Get the hell out of here."

The man flushed violently. He gestured towards Paul. "How about him?" he sputtered.

"He's in," DeNello answered coldly.

The player with the bloated face stomped angrily out of the

club. The other player, a sweatered college youth, shrugged and slid away from his seat.

Paul raised his bet to seven dollars. DeNello spoke through twisted lips. "Get your money up. No piker bets here."

Paul placed the remaining three dollars on the bet spot. "That's all this time, DeNello," he said evenly. "Take it or leave it."

In answer, DeNello broke out a new deck, shuffled the cards swiftly and handed them to Paul for the break. At least there would be a few even hands before DeNello would see the sequence, Paul mused as he split the cards.

Facing the top card under, DeNello began the deal. Paul took his first card and watched as DeNello dealt himself a card. He started suddenly as DeNello dug under the top card and handed him the second one. Then the dealer faced the top card for himself. It was a queen.

Thoughts raced through Paul's mind. DeNello had broken out a new deck. He had had no opportunity to memorize a sequence. Yet he had second-carded on his first hand. There could be only one answer. The sequence odds were not enough for DeNello in this game. He was pulling out all the stops. He was using a marked deck.

Paul glanced at his cards. A nine and a three, twelve. He faced them down on the table and drummed his fingers on the felt as if deliberating a hit. His eyes swept carefully over the deck in DeNello's hand. There were no shaves, no pin-pricks, no daubs on the top card. Paul scratched for a hit. DeNello faced the top card, a ten. Bust. As DeNello gathered in the money, Paul casually turned the ten over and groped for a cigarette. There were two incomplete diamond spots in the corner. The deck was made up of sorts.

Paul placed his wallet on the table and laid a ten-dollar bill on the bet spot. The break they had been waiting for had happened. But how could he signal Wade and Pete? If he left the club, DeNello would hide the marked deck immediately. He was certain of that. Paul deliberated about confiscating the deck himself. He glanced quickly over his shoulder at the bar. The club was empty and Danny's imposing hulk stood threateningly near.

Paul watched closely as DeNello began the deal, handing the second card off and keeping the top one for himself. Paul picked up his cards. An eight and a seven, fifteen. He glanced at De-Nello's cards. King showing. Incomplete diamonds in the corner of the down card. He had a twenty.

But the top card on the deck in DeNello's hands showed no incomplete diamonds. It was a low card. Paul scratched for a hit.

But DeNello had seen it too. He second-carded again, banking on the hope that the sharp card was a high one. It was a jack. Paul flipped his cards over.

"Bust," he muttered and placed another ten-dollar bill on the bet spot. He glanced suddenly at Pat and saw the curious expression on her face. She was looking at DeNello strangely, and Paul wondered if she had seen him cheating.

When the last bill was gone, Paul shrugged and said, "That's all I have with me, DeNello."

DeNello reached into the drawer and threw out a pad of blank checks. "You can write," he said.

It was then that the idea flashed through Paul's mind, the idea that could get him outside long enough to signal Wade and Pete. He climbed off the stool.

"I've got my own checkbook in the car," he said. "It's an out-of-town bank. Be back in a minute."

He wheeled and started toward the door. A customer had come in. He was drinking alone at the end of the bar. The man turned his head and Paul felt his stomach knot as recognition flashed into the man's eyes. It was Crosetti, the Las Vegas sharper.

Paul whipped around and moved for the twenty-one table. There was only one chance now. He would have to grab the deck himself. Crosetti's sharp voice rang through the club.

"DeNello! This guy's a gambling agent!"

The cards were lying before DeNello on the table. Paul leaped forward, his fingers groping for the deck. But at Crosetti's warning, DeNello snatched the cards away. With his free hand, he swung at Paul's head.

The blow caught Paul behind the ear. He felt a stinging, numbing tear as he rolled sideways away from the table. He turned to face the bar. Crosetti was shambling toward him, a beer bottle clutched in his hand. Behind him, Danny was locking the front door.

Paul turned again and saw Pat running toward the rear entrance. DeNello was moving forward, his hands bunched into fists. The rear entrance was the only out. Paul moved quickly toward DeNello.

As the dealer unleashed a wild punch, Paul ducked easily, smashing at DeNello's exposed stomach. He felt the blow sink in and heard a croaking, sick sound. But as he sidestepped away from the dealer, there was a stunning crash and the floor, big and unrelenting, rose up to meet him.

In a half-conscious blur, he felt the dull pain of kicks and pulled his knees up to protect himself. Then a big hand was lifting him from the floor and there was a flash of light before his eyes. And somewhere in the darkness that fell over him, there was the sound of shots.

When he opened his eyes, Pete was standing over him, slapping his face back and forth. Paul shook his head and groaned with the pain. Grasping Pete's arm, he pulled himself to his feet.

Wade was standing near them, the short-muzzled pistol in his hand. DeNello, Crosetti, and Danny were backed up against the table, their hands in the air.

"You okay, Paul?" Wade called.

"I guess so," Paul muttered through swollen lips. He moved his hand to the back of his head. It came away red with blood. "Did you get the deck?" he asked.

"What deck?" asked Wade, and DeNello laughed aloud.

"He was using sorts on me," Paul answered, weaving toward the table. He jerked open the drawer and pored through the decks. Pete moved to DeNello and searched him roughly.

DeNello laughed again. "Don't bother yourself, chumps. What you're looking for isn't here."

"It doesn't matter, DeNello," Wade said, his voice flat. "We don't need the deck. You'll never get another gambling license in this state. This little affair closes you up for good."

"Can I help it if this guy gets drunk and starts to bust up the joint?" DeNello asked with a shrug. "I got a right to throw out any stiff. My lawyer will tell you that."

Wade was silent and Paul saw the anger and frustration on his face. "Maybe, maybe not," he said. "But this place stays closed until you get a hearing." He nodded to Paul. "Let's get out of here."

Paul leaned heavily on Pete as they made their way out the front door. Wade gestured to the shattered lock. "We had to shoot the damned thing open," he said.

"How did you know I was in hot water?" Paul asked.

"Pete spotted Crosetti going in. We didn't know whether to follow him or not. We weren't sure he remembered you," Wade answered.

They stopped at the sedan and Wade opened the back door. "Get in there and lie down. We'll get you to a doctor." He reached into Paul's coat pocket and handed the keys to Pete. "Bring his car back," he said.

As the car pulled away from the club, Paul closed his eyes wearily. He turned his face to the arm cushion as they moved onto the highway. Then, suddenly, the car lurched to a quick stop. Paul raised his head. A girl was running toward the car from the darkness of the highway.

Wade rolled down the window. The girl, her face white with terror, gasped out the words. "Take me to the police! There's a man being killed in that club back there."

Wade gestured toward the back seat. "You mean that guy there?"

At the sound of Pat's voice, Paul had straightened in the seat. He grinned as her glance, stunned and uncomprehending, swung to him. Then he opened the door and grasped her by the hand. She stepped into the car wordlessly.

Her fingers were holding something and Paul raised her hand. It was a deck of cards.

"Oh, no," he moaned, not daring to hope. "Where did you get these cards?"

"He gave them to me back there," Pat said numbly.

Paul yelped aloud. Taking the deck from her hand, he dropped

it into a handkerchief and knotted it. Then he dangled the bundle
before Wade's eyes.

"Here's Mr. DeNello for you, fingerprints and all."

Wade took the bundle and carefully eased it into his pocket.
His chest heaved with a great breath. "Oh, brother. Am I going to
enjoy this," he said.

Paul leaned backward and rested against the seat. Pat turned
to face him, her eyes still wide and staring.

"I'm awfully confused, Paul," she said.

Paul clasped his hands over hers. "I'm going to take a long
time explaining," he said. "I hope you won't mind."

Pat shook her head. "I won't mind," she said.

The lights of Reno's white way loomed before them. The car
slowed as it approached the crossroads, but the signal was green,
and they sped through without stopping.

# THE

---

# MURDERER

*The wind from the winter mountains moans at the wall where I stand, and below me, the prison yard is dark and empty and silent. In a little while, it will be dawn. The eastern sky will be faint with light, but all else will be in darkness, and I will be thankful for the darkness . . .*

It was a Sunday morning, a morning for sleeping late and forgetting time, but the air that puffed in through the window was muggy and warm. The sheets on my bed had been heavy and clinging, and it hadn't helped to kick them off.

The rooming house was quiet and the stairway dim with morning gloom as I descended the carpeted steps and moved towards the door that led to the front walk. But when I reached the door, the telephone in my room began to ring, sharp and shrill through the silence of the house. I bounded up the stairs and lifted the receiver, and the shrilling stopped. It was the warden.

His voice was flat and dry. "Con got loose from the hole last night," he said. "Killed a fisherman up on Clear Creek. He used a rock."

"Yeah?"

"Know it's Sunday, but we got to get him before he makes it over the Sierra."

He didn't have to be sorry it was Sunday. He knew I needed my job. "Okay, Warden," I said. "Where's the posse?"

"There's two of them. One from below with the Indian, the tracker, and one getting ready on the highway above. You get up there and join the high one."

I paused before lowering the phone. "Warden, who is he?"

"Stewart, Paul Stewart, Washoe County, forgery, one to fourteen," he said in the same monotone. "He's got a gun. The fisherman's wife said he carried a target pistol in his fishing jacket."

"Why'd he kill the fisherman?" I asked, and was sorry I had.

There was dry amusement in the warden's voice. "Ain't you ever been in the hole?"

"No, I haven't," I answered, keeping the resentment out of my voice.

"Well, they don't wear nothing but underwear in the hole."

The phone clicked in my ear and I slammed down the receiver. Stewart, Stewart. As I pulled my boots on, I tried to place him. I was still a new enough guard not to know most of the cons. Then I remembered, remembered watching the fight from the wall, when the young con with the black hair had kicked the old man unconscious. I remembered his face when they pulled him off and led him away to the hole. He had looked more sick than mad. And Hansen had stepped out of the guard tower and said to me, "That's Stewart. Keep an eye out for him. He don't seem to like our company."

There was only a handful of cartridges in the box, four in all, and I loaded the carbine before going downstairs to the car.

The little Ford hummed along with the low, muffled roar of old Fords, and I stepped down on the gas pedal as I pulled out of the city limits and headed across the sagebrush desert. It was early morning, but the day held a promise of stifling, midday heat. The air was heavy and oppressive, but the sky was blue and clear of clouds.

At the intersection roadblock, I stopped and found out from the deputies where the second posse was forming. The Ford hummed evenly around the winding curves, and the air became cooler as I rose out of the desert furnace. But as the curves became steeper, the radiator began to heat, and water spattered back against the windshield. I stopped at a roadside fountain to cool off the engine before tackling the steeper pull to come.

By the time I reached the summit clearing, it was filled with cars but deserted of men, except for the state highway patrolman in the shiny new police car. I pulled up alongside and grinned hello, but the grin came off in a hurry.

He was slouched behind the wheel, reading the Sunday papers, and he turned his head to look me over as I drove up. He was wearing green sunglasses and a gabardine uniform.

"Whattya want, bub?"

I felt the anger rising up through my middle at the question, at the way he asked it, but I pushed it down and answered, "I'm a guard, supposed to join the posse. They gone already?"

He straightened slowly in the seat and his glance passed again over my car, which wasn't new and shiny, and me, dressed in old Levi's and a worn shirt. Then he answered, "That's right, bub. Not more'n fifteen minutes ago, right up the draw." He paused before he finished. I guess he knew I would be in trouble. "And you're too late."

This time, I didn't try to keep the anger down. All the time he was talking, I was getting madder. "The hell I am," I said and grabbed the carbine and jumped out of the car.

He opened the door of the shiny sedan. "Maybe you didn't hear me, bub. I said you're too late. I stop anybody that goes through here. Now get the hell out."

I would have gone if a whole regiment of power-drunk patrolmen had stepped out of that sedan. "I'm going, *bub.* And don't stop me." I was biting the words out as I turned my back on him and headed up the draw. I could hear him yelling. He was plenty sore, but he didn't try anything.

I was halfway up the draw, my mouth open and breathing hard, before the mad left me. I looked around then for tracks, and they weren't hard to find. A dozen men tear up the sand like a herd of horses. But at the top of the draw, it was a different matter. The sand ended and the heavy timber began. The ground was covered with a carpet of pine needles, and the tracks disappeared.

At the edge of the timber I stopped and listened for sounds from the posse, but the Sierra was silent except for the whisper of the pines and the occasional chatter of a chipmunk. On the far horizon, the tip of a thunderhead loomed dark against the blue sky.

In that silence, I had a sudden sense of misgiving. I was alone in country where armed men roamed, where some trigger-happy guard or deputy could mistake me for the convict. For the first time, I remembered that my Levi's were blue denim and hoped like hell the fisherman hadn't been wearing the same.

The smart thing to do would have been to head back for the summit clearing, but I would have cut off my legs rather than face that insulting bastard of a patrolman again, so I walked into the timber, looking sharp to right and left, ready to yell hello at a second's notice.

The country became more rugged, and silent, and the trees rose taller as I trekked deeper into the mountains. Twice, I stopped to rest, my legs aching from the long climb over the steep hillsides. My lungs burned from the closeness of the air, and looking up, I could see a thunderhead moving in swiftly. A summer storm was coming on.

The second time I stopped was on the crest of a low ridge, behind a rock, where I could blow the smoke from my cigarette into the manzanita to hide it. Every once in a long while, puffs of cool air washed down from the high snowpacks, cutting the heat and fluttering my sweat-soaked shirt. I was resting that way when I heard the crunch of footsteps.

I ground out my cigarette and smiled. Cripes, that was an achievement, moving fast enough to bypass the posse. I rose to my feet carefully with my hand raised and a call on my lips.

He was coming up the low ridge where I had been resting. The shirt was too small for him, so that it pulled tight across his chest, and the pants were too short. There was a black growth of beard on his face, and his hair hung over his ears. But I remembered him. It was Stewart.

He recoiled in surprise when I rose from behind the rock, and I saw recognition, a trapped sort of recognition, leap into his eyes.

We stood staring at each other until the first surprise melted off, and then I tried to raise the carbine, crossing it from my left hand to the right, and fumbling for the safety catch.

I hadn't meant to fire. It was just that the carbine was suddenly strange and clumsy, and I must have jerked the trigger. The discharge almost tore it loose from my hands. And the shot started it.

He went down into a crouch and reached behind him, into a hind pocket, and I saw the sun gleam on the barrel of the pistol. The air was suddenly violent with sound, and the flashes from the muzzle of the pistol flared an ugly red in the sunlight. Then I was firing too, holding the rifle before me, the butt clamped under my elbow. It bucked in my hands—one, two, three times. Then there was a pain like fire in my left leg, and I realized dimly that I had been hit. And suddenly, as swiftly as it had begun, the firing stopped.

Stewart straightened from his crouch and looked at the pistol in his hand, and then his stare lifted to me, standing on the slope above him. The pistol dropped from his fingers into the sand, and I knew it was empty. His eyes were fixed not on me, but on the muzzle of the carbine, and he raised his hands above his head in a halting, awkward gesture. I stood there for a long moment, trying to clear my head. The echoes of the shots were still ringing in my ears.

When I tried walking down the hill, the leg almost collapsed under me, and I remembered that I must have been wounded.

Bending over, I dropped my left hand to my leg, and it came away red with blood. And yet, there was no pain now, only numbing nothing, only the sickening absence of pain where pain had been. I began to retch.

When the nausea left me, I saw that Stewart was watching me curiously. His hands had dropped to his sides. I edged down the slope, moving my good leg first and swinging the other around like a prop.

"Move back," I said, and I had to say it twice. The first time, it gagged in my throat. He moved, and I picked up the pistol. It was empty, and I heaved it down the mountainside, as far as I could throw. It landed in a patch of manzanita.

"Okay, let's go," I said, motioning with the carbine down the canyon toward the summit clearing. We started, but I didn't go far. The leg was buckling, and I could tell from the warm wet on the sole of my foot that the wound was still bleeding. It was no use. I knew then I would have to wait for the posse to come. I pushed down the surge of panic that wanted to come up and told myself it would be only a little while, only a few minutes.

In a clearing at the bottom of the ridge, bounded by manzanita clumps and the tall pines, I slumped down with my back resting against a tree, ordering Stewart to do the same. He flopped down on the dirt and the pine needles, opposite me, crossing his legs like an Indian, and stared at the ground.

We sat there in silence, and I watched the blood come out of my leg. It wasn't a bad wound, but deep and to the bone, that I knew. I could hardly tell it was bleeding, except that the blood around the hole in the Levi's didn't dry, but stayed wet, and a little patch of red began to form on the pine needles. I reached for my hand-kerchief and pressed it down on the wound.

The bad leg was stretched out before me, and I balanced the rifle on the other knee, holding the stock firmly in my right hand, the muzzle pointed at Stewart's chest. I looked at him.

Something had changed him more than the uncut hair or the growth of beard. I tried to pick out what it was. And then I saw that he was gaunt, that he was even thinner than when I had seen him in the prison yard. Underneath the plaid shirt that was too small, his chest was sunken and the lines of his ribs showed. He looked up, at my leg that was bleeding, and I saw that there were deep hollows around his eyes. The pupils burned a luminous black.

He spoke for the first time. "I didn't mean to shoot you."

I just looked at him. What the hell do you say to something like that?

"I didn't, I tell you," he said. "I thought you were going to kill me." He was silent for a moment, and then he asked, "You want me to tie up your leg?"

That jolted me good. Did he think I was crazy? I stared at him and he read the surprise that showed in my eyes. He laughed a short laugh. "Tie it yourself then. You can put down the gun. I won't jump you."

I shook my head and took a tighter grip on the gun. What he was saying didn't make any sense at all.

"For Christ's sake, say something!" he spat out, and his face that had been smiling was suddenly twisted with anger. An uneasy chill went up my spine. There was something unnatural in the way his moods changed.

"It's all right," I said, and the anger on his face faded away and he smiled a slow smile. He reached down to his feet, and I straightened at the sharp movement.

He noticed it and laughed. "Take it easy. It's my feet. The shoes are too tight."

He pulled off the shoes, and I grimaced when I saw the soles of his feet. They were scraped bloody raw, as if they had been dragged across a grater. He held one shoe in his hand and looked at it.

"I guess you found the fisherman."

"I didn't. They did."

"Where are they?"

"They'll be here in a little while." I hoped like fury they would. It was sure that they'd heard the shots, the way sounds carry in the mountains, and I figured that in a while I could count on them being close and fire another shot to let them know right where I was.

And then I remembered. There weren't any spare cartridges, only the ones in the gun, and three had been fired on the slope. The truth hit me with a shock that clamped my lungs. There was only one cartridge left in the gun. The panic started to rise again, but Stewart's voice broke it.

"I didn't mean to kill him. I only wanted some shoes for my feet." He pressed his fingertips gingerly against the raw soles. "They'll gas me for this. I'll look the bastards in the eye and tell them it was an accident, that I didn't mean to kill him, and they'll laugh at me and send me to the gas chamber."

"Why'd you hit the guy?" I asked. "Did he pull the gun on you?"

Stewart shook his head. "No, it wasn't that. He forgot he even had the thing. I was just scared he'd get away, and I couldn't let him do that." He was silent for a long moment, and then he started talking, not as though he were telling it to me, but just talking. "I was lying in the sand on one side of a little rise when I saw him first, coming down the creek slow, fishing in the little pools. I wasn't going to hurt him, or even let him know I was there. I was just watching him for what he was, a man who wasn't a voice in the dark."

For an instant, I couldn't understand what Stewart meant, and then I remembered that he'd been in the hole for more than two months.

"He was a little man. He wore glasses with no rims, and his skin was pink from the sun. When he took off his hat to wipe the sweat away, there was a line where the pink ended and the bald began.

"He started to walk back up the stream, away from me, like he was going to quit fishing for the day. I laid down with my head on the sand and I began to think about going back to the hole, this time for six months, and it was a terrible thing.

"I knew the posse was close behind. I'd seen them down there this morning, down where the desert meets the mountains, and they were following something in the sand, and I knew they had my trail. I was going to give up, you know. Just lie down in the sand and wait for them to pick me up. My feet were bleeding, and the light was hurting my eyes, and the sun was burning my back.

"Then I heard the fisherman coming back. The damn fool was going to fish some more. The damn fool was coming back."

Stewart's hands knotted into tight fists, and the veins swelled at his temples. He went on.

"This time, I saw his shoes. They were the kind with the rough leather on the outside, and I could close my eyes and feel how smooth they were inside. I knew then that if I had those shoes, I could make it. I had to have them. There was a rock by my hand, and I picked it up.

"When he was real near, I stood up, and as long as I live, I'll never forget that. He pulled one hand up to his mouth, like a woman who's been scared, and his face got terrible white. I started walking for him, and he backed up and began to whimper, like a puppy. I was only going to knock him out. Then he started to run, and I couldn't let him get away."

Stewart spread his hands before him and pressed them on the ground until his fingertips disappeared into the pine needles.

"I didn't know," he said. "It wasn't until I undressed him and started to leave that I thought there was something wrong. There was blood on his head, and when I felt his heart, there was no beat. I knew he was dead, and it scared me terrible. I started to run and I went a good hundred yards before it came to me that I was running the wrong way." Stewart's voice slowed and a dead hopelessness crept into it. "I had to get away. I knew what that fisherman meant. Guys like me don't kill people, you know. They murder them."

He fell silent then and I thought about what he had said, and I knew it was true. I remembered the story I had heard about Sullivan the night before they executed him. They said he didn't know it was a cop he'd killed. He'd been in the hotel room when the plainclothesmen kicked open the door. The kid had seen them coming with guns in their hands, and he had opened up on them, thinking they were hoods from another gang. When it was over, and one cop was dead, he couldn't tell that story to anybody.

Remembering Sullivan made me remember the execution, and it wasn't good. I shook my head to kick the picture out, and when I did, the trees started to whirl in front of my eyes. I blinked and waited for things to settle back to normal. Losing all that blood was making me giddy and light-headed. I looked at the ground so that Stewart wouldn't guess what was up.

Ants, black wood ants, were crawling through the pine needles and deer flies were clustered around the handkerchief. I lifted my hand and waved them away, and I noticed that the air had become thick with insects.

Looking up, I saw that the blue had disappeared, that black clouds hung overhead. Through the trees, I could see faraway flashes of heat lightning. The air was still heavy, and closer than ever, and I knew the storm was near. I hoped the posse would come before it broke.

Stewart had pulled the shoes back on his feet, with the laces untied. I wanted to find out something, and I asked him.

"Why'd you break, Stewart?"

He shrugged. "Couldn't take it, that's all. I was going off my rocker. You know what the hole does."

I surprised him good. "No, I don't. What does it do?"

He looked at me, and his eyes were guarded. "You giving me a rough time?"

"No, dammit. I've never been in the hole."

"You really want to know what it's like?"

"Yeah."

"I'll tell you," Stewart said, and his voice got low. "There's no light in the hole. Only darkness. You lay in your cell with nothing on but your underwear, but you don't need clothes because it's hot as the insides of hell. When you first go down, you lay flat on the cement and you think your lungs are going to burst, because there's no air. You lay still and feel your heart kicking against your ribs, and pretty soon, you faint.

"When you come to, you can hear yourself moaning. And the other cons laugh, and one of them, Conyer, giggles because he's out of it. But it's okay. You get used to it after a while. But when you think you are used to it, you notice that your legs are cramped from not moving. So you get up and try walking back and forth in your cell. Just one trip and you pass out again. And when you come to this time, you know better and lay quiet on the cement.

"You lay on the cement because there's no cot in your cell. There's nothing in your cell except a bucket. You do it in a bucket and live with your own stink."

I thought I was going to be sick. I was still shaky and Stewart's story wasn't making things any better. He went on.

"But the terrible thing is the darkness. Darkness all the time until the guard comes down, once in the day and once in the night, and shoves your bread and soup into your cell. And all the time he's there, you watch his flashlight and keep your eyes on it like it was a last hope, and you're sick with longing for it when he leaves."

Stewart paused, and a chipmunk scurried into the clearing. He stopped between us and sat up, and then fled for cover when Stewart started speaking again.

"There was one screw who knew how much we loved that light, how we loved it like a woman.

"He'd come down the steps backward, hiding the light from us so there was barely enough for himself to see. And he'd shove our food under our doors and walk over by the stairway and blink it off, and we'd scream at him that someday, we'd kill him for it.

"Once, I made a mistake. By counting the guard's visits, I'd been keeping track of when it was day and when it was night outside. It was terrible important to me, to know that. One time, I got twisted up on the visits, and I had to know, so I asked the screw. He told me it was day outside, and I forgave him every-thing. I could have kissed his feet.

"But when he got back to the steps, he looked back and said, 'By God, I can't remember. It might be night after all.' And then he went away, and I laid there and cried, I was so sick."

"Who was he?" I asked, and I thought I knew the answer.

"Beasley," Stewart answered. "And as long as I live, I'll be-lieve he was the bastard that put the old guy up to it."

"What do you mean?"

"The guy I beat up in the yard. I saw Beasley talking to him just a little while before. And then the old guy propositions me. God, I wanted to beat his brains out." Stewart's face had the sick look on it that I remembered from the yard.

I could believe it was Beasley, all right. He was the one who taught me that sadists don't always look like lean, hollow-eyed men with dead eyes and cold lips. He taught me that sadists can come in fat bodies with big stomachs and fleshy hands. He taught me that sadists come in pasty-white faces with slack jaws and thick lips and pig eyes. And he taught me that sadists can laugh.

I knew him for my first week in the yard, when he asked the warden to let me help him with the Sullivan execution, and I had to do it because it was an order.

I remembered standing in death row with Beasley and waiting for the kid to come out. When we opened the door, he was sitting on the edge of his cot with his head in his hands, and when he looked up, his face was white.

And I remembered Beasley laughing thick in his throat and saying, "Don't be scared, boy. It'll be over in a little while." And Williams, who was in the cell next to the kid's, jumped to the bars and threw his coffee at Beasley, and swore, "You rotten son-of-a-bitch," and he said every word of it slow.

Beasley's face had gone dead gray, and his jaw hung slacker, and he wiped the coffee off his face and said, "I'll be around when it's your time."

Then we were walking out of death row with the "Goodbye, Davy" calls following us down the corridor, and when we walked across the prison yard in the dark of dawn, I was shivering with more than the cold.

When we got inside the chamber, the kid walked over to the white chair and sat down, and Beasley tied his legs and I looped the strap across his chest. I could see that he was shying away from Beasley, as if he could sense something evil in him. And then he looked up at me, and he tried to say something, but his lower lip began to tremble, and his eyes were big and black with fear. Then he clenched his mouth shut and closed his eyes, and never opened them again until we had gone out and sealed the door, and I never knew what he wanted to say.

When he was dead and the fumes had fogged up the windows, I was still staring and it was like a bad dream. Then I heard Beasley's laugh behind me, and he said, "Step inside, boy, and wipe off the windows so's we can see."

Stewart's voice jerked me back to the clearing, and I was thankful. "You got a smoke?" he asked. "There's no cigarettes in the hole either."

I reached into my shirt pocket and pulled one out of the pack and flipped it to him. But after I had thrown the matches, I fell back against the tree, because the movement had sent my head reeling again. The trees blurred and spun, and somewhere far back in my mind, something began to bother me, but I couldn't reach it. It was like being in a crowded room and listening to a conversation you can't quite hear.

When my vision cleared, Stewart was smoking. He drew the smoke deep into his lungs and let it out easy. For the first time, he leaned back against the tree behind him.

"The guy who said the first cigarette in a long time tastes lousy was crazier than hell."

I tried to keep talking. "Stewart, did you crawl out the sewer tunnel?"

He nodded.

"Where'd you get the saw?"

He grinned, and then he laughed out loud. "You're not that new of a screw. You know better than to ask that."

I felt like a little kid who's been told he knows better, and it made me mad. After that, I kept my mouth shut. Instead, I lit myself a cigarette, but the first drag made me dizzy again, and I laid my head back against the rough bark of the tree until it cleared. My arms were beginning to feel weighted, my mind logy, and I knew I was getting weaker every minute.

Stewart was staring at me, his eyes wrinkled up in a frown. He seemed to be trying to remember something.

"Where's the posse?" he asked finally, in a voice that was too casual.

I sensed trouble. "They'll be here."

The frown was still there. "Why don't you fire a shot to let them know where we are?"

I slid my left hand forward on the barrel of the gun. "Never mind," I said. "They'll find us."

Stewart didn't answer. He sat there cross-legged and unmoving for a moment, and then he uncrossed his legs and rose to one knee.

"I got a hunch that gun is empty. I haven't seen you load it." He started to rise to his feet.

I lifted the rifle and aimed it at his chest. But when I fingered for the trigger, he sat down suddenly, letting his feet go out from under him. I lowered the gun, wondering why I was sorry he hadn't tried to jump me.

"No, I guess you've got one left at that," he said, crossing his legs again and picking up a pine needle from the ground. "It's a funny thing. Here I am, sure to get gassed anyway, and yet, I'm afraid to take a chance on getting killed. What the hell is there in a man that makes him act that way?"

I didn't answer. The exertion of lifting the rifle had sapped out what little was left of my strength. The trees and the sky and Stewart were whirling before me, and then something dark tipped over me, and there were flashes of light in the darkness. When it all faded away and things were straight again, I knew that the next one would be the one that would lay me out cold in front of Stewart. And I knew quite suddenly what I had to do. It was like hearing something you've always known, but never hearing it in words before. I had to shoot him.

But when I said it to myself, it didn't hit right. It sounded wrong as hell, like I was doing terrible wrong. If I did faint, maybe he would only take the gun and keep on going. Oh hell, yes! Who was I kidding? He'd already murdered once that day. He'd make sure I wouldn't come to in time to sound out to that posse. He knew as well as I did that they'd be blanketing the area in a little while, and that if they didn't find me, they wouldn't know where his trail began. No, Stewart would fix that. He'd ditch my body so they'd play hell finding it, but I wouldn't care. I'd be dead.

Then why did I feel wrong about shooting him? One shot would do the trick, would kill him and signal the posse right to the spot in one whack. That's all there would be to the thing. But why couldn't I do it? Because he'd told me how it was he'd killed the fisherman? Because he was helpless and I couldn't kill him in cold blood?

I couldn't be sure. I couldn't be sure. And I was afraid, more afraid than I'd ever been in my life. That was enough. At least I could never know that he wouldn't have killed me. At least I could have that satisfaction. It wasn't much, but goddam, it was enough.

When I looked up again, all the insects had disappeared. The clearing was silent as nothing had been that day. The sky was dark, and there was a rumble of thunder over the mountains.

Stewart had stuffed out his cigarette in the sand, beneath the pine needles. "Got another smoke?" he asked. "Guess I'm a chainer."

I reached into my pocket and flipped him the whole pack, and then the matches. I looked at his chest, to the right of where the shirt came to a V. It would have to be there. He would never know what happened. Slowly, I moved my right foot back, raising my knee and the rifle at the same time.

The cigarettes landed short, and Stewart leaned forward to reach for them. I aimed the rifle. The front sight centered on his chest, below the V. But I couldn't pull the trigger! I couldn't do it!

And then, as Stewart settled back, I felt the darkness coming over me again, far back and slow, and I knew I was going out. I raised my head. Stewart was fumbling with the pack. He pulled out a cigarette and placed it between his lips. It dangled there while he reached for the matches. I raised the rifle again and moved my left hand forward on the barrel. The front sight swung into line, to the right and below the V, where his heart was. Dimly, I heard the scratch of the match on the box. Then I pulled the trigger.

The click sounded louder than a cannon through the silence of the clearing. My head reeled. The gun was empty! The gun was empty! And then it came to me. I had forgotten the first shot on the slope, the shot that had started the shooting. I had miscounted.

Stewart's head snapped up at the sound. He sat there, the cigarette hanging loosely from his lips, staring at me. Then, slowly, the realization of what had happened came into his eyes. He rose to his feet, and I fell back against the tree. My hands dropped, and the gun slid away into the pine needles.

The darkness was very close and I could not raise my eyes. Through the mist, the man that was Stewart approached me. Then he was standing over me, and I couldn't move as I waited for the blow to come. But there was none. Only a furious, flat voice. A voice that said, "And I'm the lousy murderer," and was gone.

There was the sound of fading footsteps in the sand, and overhead, the sky crackled with lightning. And then, the darkness came down over me and blotted out the awful sickness that was in me.

There was a pressure on my leg and the raw taste of whiskey in my throat when I awoke. It was raining. A fine spray washed through the pine boughs above me and onto my face. I grasped the arm that held me and pulled myself to a sitting position.

The clearing was filled with men, armed men, and at the far edge, his arms tied behind him, the rain dripping from his black hair, stood Stewart.

He stood with his back to me.

# THE

## SNAKE

### PEN

Smale Calder slid the ill-fitting black coat from his bulging shoulders, grunted as he jerked at the bulky knot in the tie, and began fumbling at the buttons to his shirt.

He was standing at the foot of the bed, and Jenny stole a quick, sidled glance at him through the mirror. The skin of his upper body was whiter than his face. She had not believed it was possible. Quite without knowing why, she thought of the snake pen.

Even though the white frilled collar of the wedding dress hung loosely about her thin neck, she craned her head upwards, first to the right and then to the left, trying to breathe through the tightness in her throat. Her heart was beating wildly, and she instinctively placed a hand to her breast. The motion made her cast another sideward glance, at his hands. They were short and square, and in spite of all the scouring he had done for the wedding, they were still rutted in the creases with black grease. Jenny pulled her hand down from her breast as though she had touched fire.

She was standing with her back to the bed and to him. More than three times, she had set the small bouquet of flowers on the dresser and picked them up again. They were wilted by the close heat of all the bodies that had jammed their way into her father's grease-smelling farmhouse. Jenny thought with satisfaction of the day and all its confusion. For the first time in as long as she could remember, she had been the center of attention, she and Smale Calder. Even her father had looked at her without his usual concealed distaste, and she had even felt pretty in a way. Once, during the party, she had escaped from the crowd and forced her way into the smelly bathroom to look into the mirror. The white veil at least had hidden her protruding front teeth. Why had she been wished such teeth when her mother's were so small and straight, and even her father, Amelio, could smile a fine, even smile, even though his teeth were big in his mouth?

The tiny, threaded knots in the white veil had hidden the dark, sagging pouches beneath her eyes, in fact, had hidden the whole of her round face. She had felt quite satisfied, standing in the bathroom, breathing through her mouth so that she could stand the smell, staring into the mirror.

A door slammed shut in the silent house and Jenny started suddenly. She turned and saw that she was alone. Smale Calder had gone into the bathroom. She plucked nervously at the lower button on her right sleeve, and when it pulled loose, her heart thumped, hurting in her chest. She raised her wrist for help, but thought of Calder's grease-rutted hands and fumbled instead for the second button on her sleeve. It came loose and her heart thumped again, but this time it was with a pang almost of pleasure. She wondered idly if it were because Smale Calder was not in the room.

She wondered too at the small pricks of resentment against her father. Had he been too willing to marry her off, to anyone, it seemed? When she thought back, she remembered the day she had driven with Amelio in his truck to Calder's garage. She had slid out of the front seat, and her skirt had caught on the loose spring sticking through the seat, and her legs had been exposed all the way to her thighs. Smale Calder had been filling the gas tank, and he had seen it, and he had raised his eyes and stared at her as if seeing her for the first time. Amelio had seen it too, and from then on, Jenny remembered, Amelio insisted that she drive with him whenever he took the trip from the farm to Calder's garage for gasoline or repairs.

And for the first time in her life, Calder began to speak to her. As well as he knew how, at any rate. For Smale Calder never spoke more than a few words to any man. He was that way, guttural and brief. Finally, he had paid court at the farm, and they had sat, all of them, in the grease-smelling main room of the farmhouse and drunk wine. Jenny had perched stiffly on the old sofa, the fingers of her right hand self-consciously over her buck teeth, and Calder had sat beside her, talking to Amelio. When the evening was done, he had still said only hello to Jenny, and then he said goodbye, and left.

A week later they were married, and all the Italian farmers in the whole community had dressed in their black best and driven to Amelio's in their old trucks, with the racks stained with manure and hay, and gotten uproariously drunk on wine. And she had, at least, felt some satisfaction when the party was done, when Calder held open the car door for her and they had driven away, amidst all the sly and not so sly gibes from the guests. Except for the priest's, it was the only car there.

Jenny heard the toilet flush, and she pulled nervously at the buttons on the other sleeve. Perhaps it would be like the times with Elio, the hired hand on the farm. She remembered that in the last week before the wedding, that day when Elio began mucking out the ditches in the far field, she had tried to resist. It seemed to be the right thing to do, what with the wedding coming up in less than a week. She had handed Elio the flour sack with the pot of stew and the bread and the wine in it, and had turned to go, but he had reached up from the ditch and caught her by the hand. His smile had been white and even too.

"Hey! What for you go so quick?"

"Work. I gotta work. I gotta get my dress ready. Mamma's taking it out of the trunk today."

"Stay. I do not like to eat alone. You can talk to me."

And she had relented. And Elio had pulled her down on the hay stubble behind the willow patch. And when it was done, she had gone back across the fields to the house, and Elio ate his lunch alone anyway. Jenny remembered that his shoulders were brown with the sun.

The door to the bedroom opened and Smale Calder came in, his feet bare, dressed only in his trousers. A look of irritation flickered briefly in his black eyes. He had a tremendous breadth of chest and shoulders, on which his head sat like a small bud on a great branch. His skin was always white, thick and white, and his short hair lay lank and flat to the skull, like a cap.

"You want a drink?"

Jenny swallowed past the tightness in her throat. It seemed a strange question to ask now. She shook her head.

"It ain't any of that goddam vino. It's whiskey."

Jenny nodded. "Okay."

When he left the bedroom again, Jenny breathed a deep breath and began to undress swiftly. She would be in bed by the time he came back in. That would be better than having him watch her undress. Jerking off the mothball-smelling dress, she draped it over the chair and began to dig at her silk stockings. She was naked, shoving her arms through the nightgown, when he came back in. She saw the look flicker across his eyes—the same look she had seen when her dress caught on the spring—and she jerked on the nightgown hurriedly, twisting it right. She wondered why he never blinked.

They sat on the edge of the bed, sipping their drinks. Jenny shivered. The room seemed cold with its bare stucco walls. At least the farmhouse had been warm, even if it always smelled of grease and wine. But the whiskey was warm, and by the time the drink was through, she even felt a little giggly.

"More goddam vino," Calder was saying. "I never knew there was so goddam much vino in the world." He took the glasses and moved into the kitchen. Jenny jerked back the covers and crawled into bed. Calder came back into the bedroom and switched off the lights, and she could hear him pulling off his trousers in the darkness. She was glad the room was dark.

He rose early in the morning and Jenny could hear him fixing his breakfast in the kitchen. She thought she should get up and help him, but by the time she poked a foot out of the covers, he had banged out through the kitchen door on his way to the garage. Jenny pulled her foot back into the warmth of the bed, stirred languorously, and closed her eyes. It had been altogether a satisfactory night, and she was sleepily tired.

There were times in which Jenny did not regret her marriage. Calder's house, built by himself in the little crossroads cluster of buildings that marked the center of the farming community, was by far the best house in town. A white frame building, it boasted three rooms, not counting the bathroom, and a front porch. Calder did a thriving business in the garage, even more than he could really handle by himself. It kept him out of the house almost all day, every day. He came in only for lunch and supper. And he was good to her. Not to the extent of overtures of goodness, but he did not beat her like Amelio had done to her mother. He merely left her alone, and during the day, Jenny could appreciate this.

From the kitchen window, she watched the people go by and grimaced. They were on their way to the snake pen in the yard between the garage and the house. Calder would enter the pen today, and they came like vultures to watch him.

Smale Calder was famous for what he could do with snakes. Once, a magazine had sent a writer to check on the stories that found their way into the newspaper in the county seat, ten miles away. The writer had come with a knowing, skeptical air, but the skepticism, as well as his color, had vanished by the time he left. The article appeared in the magazine, and Calder had been proud—until he looked up the word the writer had used to describe him. The writer had called him reptilian.

Once, on the first day after the wedding, Jenny had ventured into the yard to watch him. She never went back again.

Calder had waited until the people grouped around the tight wire mesh of the snake pen had settled comfortably. Then he had opened the gate and closed it quietly behind him. The rattle-snakes, a dozen of them, all sprawled basking in the sun, their eyes eternally open and unblinking, had all coiled as one. They had arched their necks and cocked their spade heads low, the forked, black threads flickering out of their mouths, their tails buzzing together until the air was filled with a death-dry rattle. A shiver had coursed up Jenny's spine, and for an instant, she was afraid for Calder. And the people, their faces empty and emotion-less and stripped of the masks they wore, had tensed. Jenny had felt that tension, felt it emanate from their bodies and fill the yard until it seemed it would smother her.

Then Calder had walked to the center of the pen, and the buzz-ing had grown unbelievably louder. He stood there, immobile as a statue, his black eyes roving over the snakes. Then, almost im-perceptible in its changing, the buzzing had quieted until it was a low hum, and still Calder stood motionless, only his eyes moving. Time had stretched into eternity, and the midday heat poured down on the pen, rising from the baked earth in stifling waves. Finally, even the hum faded away.

Then she saw the thing of which she had heard since she was a child. She knew what was to happen, and yet it was terrible to her. The snakes had uncoiled slowly, their heads slithering over their coils onto the sand, and they had come to Calder like chicks to a mother hen. He had knelt in the sand of the snake pen, and they coiled on his arms, and his legs, and he had twined them about his neck, and a woman had screamed and fainted, but the snakes didn't buzz. Calder stroked their heads and their undersides with his short, square fingers, and they had curled lazily and sensu-ously about him.

The sun was hot in the summer's day and the heat had hung heavily in the yard, but Jenny, shaking with the cold, had run inside the house and vomited.

Jenny was still in the kitchen when the people trooped back past the window, some with their faces still white and drawn, others shaking their heads and smiling stiffly in disbelief, and others with their lips twisted in revulsion.

The kitchen door banged and Jenny wheeled around. Calder had come in. He was standing with one hand resting against the kitchen table. His shoulders were slumped forward and there were lines of fatigue around his eyes. His lips were parted and his jaw hung slack.

It had been like this once before. "What's the matter?" Jenny asked.

"I'm tired. Think I'll go to bed for a little while," Calder answered heavily. He lifted his hand from the table and moved slowly towards the bedroom, then stopped. "Will you close up the garage? The key's by the gas pump." He moved away.

"Smale?"

He stopped in the doorway without turning. "Yes."

Jenny braced herself. "Why don't you get rid of the snakes?"

He turned ponderously and stared at her. "What?"

"Get rid of those snakes. They're making you sick. I'm worried about you."

Surprise showed in his gray face, almost a pleasant surprise. "That's nice, Jenny."

"Will you?"

"No." He turned away slowly and moved into the bedroom, closing the door behind him.

Jenny had learned what to expect from the time before. She ate her dinner alone, and when it was late, she crawled into bed. Calder was breathing heavily in deep sleep. Jenny's bare foot touched his leg and she pulled it away quickly. She lay in bed, eyes open, staring unseeingly into the darkness. It had been so long.

But the bridge was made. Jenny, spurred on by her first bold request about the snakes, and by the irritation that kept her from sleep in the nights, continued to goad him. Calder listened to her pleas and her demands placidly, then said "No" gently, and the argument was dropped until the next time.

Jenny gave up, and, tortured by her loneliness, went to visit her mother. She arrived at the farmhouse in the morning. The timing was purposeful, even though she would not admit it to herself. When lunchtime came, she volunteered with a desperate casualness to carry the lunch to Elio in the far field. Her mother declined the offer smilingly, and Jenny almost cried. But when the mother turned to tend the bread baking in the oven, Jenny took the lunch and left quickly across the fields. She gave herself up to Elio with a hunger that startled the farmhand. Never having known marriage, he wondered briefly if all the stories he had heard were untrue, and that perhaps, by order of the Church, relations ceased after marriage. Then he remembered his own birth and dismissed the thought. After all, his mother had been a saintly woman.

Jenny came back that afternoon to Calder's house and discreetly refrained from singing as she prepared supper. Even Calder wondered why she failed to bring up the argument about the snakes.

It happened on a day when Calder was busy under a car in the garage, and while Jenny was baking bread.

The two sons of Gino Gondi, who owned the grocery store near Calder's garage, had begun an argument concerning the snake pen. Gino the younger, who had watched Calder's eyes pass over the snakes whenever he entered the pen, argued that eyes were the secret of Calder's success. And since he himself possessed eyes that were almost black, at least a deep brown, he maintained that he could also charm the snakes. The younger brother, Alfred, laughed aloud, and Gino fumed.

He volunteered to submit to the test. And when no one was looking, and as Alfred stood by at a safe distance, Gino unlatched the pen gate and stepped inside, his heart in his mouth and his bare legs tingling with fear. When the realization came that he had made a mistake, he was too numbed to move. The snakes slithered toward him, but they stopped and coiled before they reached him.

Alfred watched in horror as the spade heads sprang from the coils and fastened onto his brother's legs. He watched in silent horror as his brother opened his mouth to scream, but could not utter a sound. Finally, when Gino slid to the ground amid a mass of dusty coils, Alfred ran away. He crossed the dirt street and raced through the back door of the grocery and into his bed. A half hour later, his mother found him there, still shaking and sobbing, and forced the story from his lips.

Calder was the one who removed the child's body from the snake pen, but the people were little grateful. That afternoon, the undersheriff, who lived in the county seat, drove to the community and ordered Calder to kill the snakes. Calder refused, and the undersheriff reached into his car, produced a shotgun, and shouldered past Calder into the yard where the snake pen stood. In the kitchen, Jenny listened as the booming shots sounded at regular intervals. She counted twelve, and smiled. And inside the garage, where he stood with helplessly clenched fists, Calder's huge frame recoiled with every shot.

That night, Calder ate no dinner. He sat at the kitchen table, under the light of the single glaring bulb that hung from the ceiling, and drank his whiskey. Jenny gently tried to make him eat.

"Smale, you gotta eat. You shouldn't drink on an empty stomach."

"Not hungry," Smale muttered, staring blankly at the shining globules the overhead light showed in the whiskey.

"Please try to eat."

"Not hungry, goddam it. Leave me alone."

"I'm sorry," Jenny said defensively.

Calder was instantly solicitous. "I'm sorry, Jenny. I didn't mean it." He reached across the table and patted her hand. It was warm. Calder looked at Jenny. It had been a long time, he thought. Jenny knew the look and she ate her dinner casually and quickly. When she was through, she left the dishes on the table and followed Calder into the bedroom. But this time it was Calder's hunger that rose up to meet hers, and meeting it, overwhelmed it with a raging passion. Jenny slept dreamlessly until the afternoon of the next day, and when she awoke, she was still tired.

It was a week before Jenny visited her mother at the farmhouse again. She came in the morning, but only through necessity, since

Calder needed the car in the afternoon. When lunchtime came, she commented with fervor about her mother's turned ankle, saying there was nothing she could do, she would have to take Elio's lunch to him in the far field.

She trekked across the hay stubble reluctantly, handed Elio his sack, and turned away. Elio laughed and caught her by the hand. She wheeled and slapped him soundly across the face. Elio dropped her hand and stepped back, his mouth open and his fingers to his stinging cheek, and Jenny walked away. Elio sat down on the edge of the ditch and reached absently for the sack. He was confused.

For the first time in her married life, the hours of afternoon began to slip by too swiftly for Jenny's liking. Dinner was upon her hardly before she was aware that she had risen from her bed. She lingered over her plate long after Calder had finished. She read until she could keep her eyes open no more, and then she went to bed. Calder never said anything, but he was always awake and waiting when she came. She gave herself up helplessly to his insatiable lust. She began to lose weight, despite the fact that she was already thin to the point of being scrawny. She hoped desperately that she would become pregnant.

It was a drowsy afternoon in early autumn, and the cottonwoods that shaded the cluster of houses in the community were hazy with a gentle light. Jenny, a magazine in her hand, trudged wearily from the house onto the porch. She noticed that the sun was sinking rapidly behind the cottonwoods and knew that nightfall would soon descend over the fields. She sighed and sank into the wicker chair. Her eyes noted listlessly a movement in the ivy that graced the side of the porch.

When the spade head and the flickering tongue slid from beneath a red-tinted leaf, the magazine slipped from her fingers. She felt the blood drain from her face, and her legs turn to stone, and she knew that she must move. The snake slid silently onto the wooden floor of the porch, and she saw the diamond pattern on its back. Then, from the garage behind, an exhaust banged. The noise broke the spell. She leaped from the wicker chair and screamed. The snake whipped into a coil, its tail buzzing, but Jenny was already racing blindly through the door, her screams shattering the drowsy silence of the afternoon.

She was standing in the kitchen, her hands to her head, screaming, when Calder's huge bulk rammed through the kitchen door. He grasped her by the shoulders and shook her.

"What's the matter, Jenny? What the hell's the matter?"

She continued to scream, and Calder cuffed her across the face. The blow cut her scream, and she stood staring at him.

"What the hell's the matter, goddam it, Jenny?"

"Snake," she managed to whisper. "Snake on the porch."

It was the first time she ever saw Calder blink. It was a slow blink, his thin lids sliding over his black eyes. He released his grasp and shouldered past her.

"Smale!" she called.

He turned. "Yeah?"

"Kill him, *please!*"

He turned away, and Jenny collapsed on the kitchen chair, her face in her hands, sobbing. She cried until she heard the kitchen door open, and then she raised her head. Her eyes were red-rimmed.

"Did you kill him?"

Calder moved toward the kitchen sink and began to wash the grease from his hands.

"Don't worry. I got rid of him."

When he came to sit at the table, Jenny rose wearily and began to prepare the meal. She looked outside and saw that the sun had disappeared behind the mountains. It was almost night, and she was dreadfully tired. She tried not to think of the night.

She loitered through her dinner again, but Calder ate swiftly. Her mouth set in rigid lines when he rose, wiped his mouth with the back of one hand, set the napkin down on the table, and moved towards the bedroom.

"Take your time, Jenny," he muttered. "I think I'll go ahead."

She lingered over the plate until it was cold, then emptied it, and lingered over the second plate. Finally, when the dishes were done, she dragged herself into the bedroom. She stopped at the side of the bed, her eyes wide in surprise when she heard his heavy breathing. Calder was asleep.

A week slipped by, and Jenny gained back her weight. She even added two pounds and thought perhaps she might be pregnant, but when the time came, she knew she had been wrong. The week was pleasant, and Calder always went to bed early. But when the second week passed, Jenny began to be restless. She thought of visiting her mother, but then she remembered that the ditchwork was alway finished by autumn, so she stayed at home. She tried to read, was bored, and sewed. Finally, she decided to take a chance and eat dinner at the same speed as Calder.

They finished at the same time, and Jenny followed him into the bedroom. He undressed and crawled into bed, turned over, and went immediately to sleep. Jenny lay in the darkness, her eyse open. A nameless fear had entered her mind, but she did not know what it was.

When the third week passed, Jenny was desperate. Calder treated her as always, but always he was tired. She watched as he finished dinner, rose, and entered the bedroom. This time, he closed the door behind him.

Jenny sat at the table for a long time. Her eyes roved over the silent kitchen and fastened on the key to the garage, hanging on a nail by the door, and the fear returned. She stared at it for a moment, then turned her eyes away and poured herself a cup of coffee. She was raising the cup to her lips when her eyes caught on the key again. It was rimmed with silver in the glaring light from the lone bulb. She shook her head and closed her eyes as she drank the coffee.

But when it was time to go to bed, she reached for the cord that hung from the bulb and saw the key again. Her hand dropped and she stared at the key for a long time. Then she walked to the door and took it down from the nail. She listened at the bedroom door, heard Calder's heavy breathing, and rummaged in the corner of the utensil drawer until she found the flashlight.

The night was cool, and she clasped her arms across her breasts as she moved through the yard. The community was going to bed, and the lights were blinking off one by one in the cluster of houses.

She walked through the darkness to the garage door and opened it. The smell of oil-soaked boards assailed her nostrils as she entered, and the flashlight poked a cone of light into the darkness. She stopped once and tried to shake the thing from her mind, but it would not go. She began to walk about in the garage, flashing the light to right and left before her. She passed the bins of nails and screws, past the vise and the locks. She skirted the corner of the garage, saw the light catch on a section of wire mesh that protruded from a bin below the worktable, and turned away. Then she remembered the wire mesh, and she turned back.

There was a handle with which to pull the bin open, and it was from the crack above the handle that the wire mesh showed. She shoved the flashlight closer and wondered why her chest was constricted so that she could hardly breathe. She moved closer to the bin. Behind her, the garage door thudded shut. She wheeled, one hand to her mouth, the other aiming the flashlight at the door. There was no one there. She felt herself grow limp with relief, and she turned back to the bin.

But the handle was fastened by a tiny steel chain, a chain that looped underneath the worktable. She stooped down and played the light on the underside of the table. The end of the chain was linked to the boards by a heavy lock.

Jenny straightened and stood uncertainly in the darkness. Then she stepped forward and kicked the tin bottom of the bin gently with her toe. There was no sound. She kicked again, hard, so that the tin boomed. This time, she heard it, heard the dry, furious buzzing that echoed from the sides of the bin, muffled and hollowed by the tin. She recoiled, her mouth open to scream, and then she clapped her hand to her mouth and stepped away.

After a long time, she stepped out through the garage door, fastened the lock, and went back to the house. She closed the kitchen door behind her quietly, put away the flashlight, and hung up the key. Then she sat down. The lone bulb glared down on the table, and she stared at the empty coffee cup. There was a stain on the side where the coffee had dripped. She shivered. She was terribly frightened, but she did not know why.

# THE
---
# FIRST
---
# SNOW

In the beginning, the figure of the old man was an uncertain shade in the darkness of the long street, moving slowly forward, out of the night and falling snow.

Beneath the dangling street lamp there was an arc of light into which the snow swirled silently and crazily from the night above, and the light reached out and touched the approaching figure and its hat and coat of shapeless black.

The old man shambled slowly into the light, his head bent to the softly pelting snow. His path was marked by slender swaths in the whiteness of the sidewalk. He moved so slowly that when he paused beneath the swaying lamp, and looked to right and left along the deserted street, it seemed that he had always been there beneath the light. But when he stepped into the street and crossed, with the tiny, tedious movements of a child, out of the arc of light, it was as though he had never been there at all.

He shuffled past the dark storefronts but did not turn his head. He moved past them with an old familiarity, as though they had always been dark, and as though he knew they should have been so.

The high, old windows of the saloon were filled with a light that was dim and warm, and when the old man came to the door, he drew both hands from the pockets of the black coat and turned the knob, then pushed inward and sidled through the narrow aperture he had made.

Except for the barkeeper, the saloon was empty. A single globe hung down from the ceiling, angling its light over the bar and the shining glasses, and pushing the darkness upwards to the corners of the ceiling.

But the weak rays did not reach even to the end of the bar. Beyond that, the long room was thick with gloom, pinpointed only by shafts of light from a potbellied stove. Around the stove stood three empty chairs.

The old man moved close to the bar and unbuttoned the black coat. Pulling it off slowly, he shook off the snow that mantled its shoulders. Then he removed the hat and brushed the flakes from its rim with stiff movements of his fingers.

There seemed to be no flesh on his face. The skin was stretched tight over sharp cheekbones and the bladed ridge of his nose. In the light from the single globe, his eyes, shining and wet, were sunken deep into dark sepulchers. It seemed that his thin, almost indefinable lips could never have known color.

He brushed his wispy white hair down flat on his head. "Evening, Billy."

"Evening, Tom," the barkeeper answered gently. He shifted on a stool and rested a newspaper on his lap. But he looked away when the old man turned his head to peer into the gloom that shrouded the end of the saloon.

There was a silence, and the old man turned and followed the barkeeper's gaze to the high windows. The snow was beginning to fall more heavily.

"First snow," the barkeeper murmured.

The old man nodded. "First snow," he echoed. There was a pause, and then he added, "It's a pretty thing."

They watched the falling snow together, until they seemed to have been caught in a spell. They watched with unmoving, with leveled, staring eyes, until the deep tones of the clock above the door broke the spell.

The old man raised his head and looked at the clock. "Pretty late," he mumbled almost inaudibly. He glanced again at the end of the long room, and a shadow, almost of doubt, crossed his face.

The barkeeper watched him for an instant and then picked up his newspaper. "There's a storm tonight, Tom," he said.

The old man glanced at him quickly, guardedly, but the barkeeper did not raise his eyes from his reading. The old man pondered for a moment, then nodded his head slowly. "That's right. There's a storm tonight," he said. "Guess I'll go sit by the fire for a bit, Billy."

The barkeeper watched him go, then laid the newspaper down on his lap again and stared at the falling snow.

The old man shuffled to a stop beside a long board on the wall and hung his hat and coat on one hook. Then he turned and moved towards the stove. Grasping the worn side arms of the center chair, he lowered himself slowly. He leaned forward and held his open palms to the warmth, opening and closing his fingers stiffly. Then he sat back in the chair and stretched out his legs.

Through one of the chinks, he could see a mad flame dancing in the grate. He watched it and listened to the rustle of the wood chunks as they settled in the stove.

Once, he straightened in the chair and turned to look back towards the light, and again, the furrow crossed his brow. Shaking his head, he settled back. After a while, his gaze roved to the other chairs, but he looked away quickly, as though there were something he did not want to see. But his glance crept to them again, and finally he rose and dusted off their seats with his sleeve. Then he returned to his chair.

He seemed not to hear the clock toll the half-hour, but sat motionless, the mad flame writhing in reflection upon his aged face.

When he felt the hand upon his shoulder, he started involuntarily. Half raising himself in the chair, he looked confusedly to right and left.

"Evening, Tom."

"Evening, Iver. Evening, John," the old man said tremulously. "Sit down. Sit down. I'm glad you come. It was getting so late, I didn't think you were coming at all. Was it the storm held you up? It was the storm, I bet."

"It was the storm."

Tom nodded eagerly and sat down again in the chair, his eyes shining. "I knew it was. I knew it was. I had trouble myself tonight, what with the path being so slippery with the snow, and the night so dark. I truly thought of turning back." He stretched his legs out in front of him and glanced to left and right, smiling. Finally, he rested his clasped hands in his lap.

On the small window beside the stove, the snow brushed quietly in a ceaseless whisper. The falling flakes, arrested suddenly on the pane, held intact but for a moment, then faded crystal by crystal until they were gone. But in their wake was a wetness that shone long after they had vanished.

"The first snow. It's such a pretty thing."

Tom turned his head and nodded slowly. "It is that, Iver. It is that." Unclasping his hands, he rested them on the arms of the chair. "Before you come in, I was sitting here thinking. You know, Iver, and you, John, we ain't missed a first snow together as long as I can remember. Why, I recall us watching it together as far back as when we was young ones in school. Do you remember, Iver?"

"I remember, Tom."

The smile was still warm in Tom's eyes. "It's a strange thing, but even now, as old as I be, the sight of it makes me feel that I must be about something, that I must go somewhere."

He hesitated for an instant, as though uncertain whether to go on. Then he relaxed in the chair and continued.

"When we was kids, and the first flakes come out of the sky and past the window, we fidgeted in our seats like fire. I recall Miss Heritage saying over and over again, 'Now, quit your fidgeting. You just quit your fidgeting. When your time in here is done, you can go out to the snow, but not before.'"

"Finally, the time come, and we could run out of the school-house and shout and yelp, and heave snowballs at each other, and roll in the white stuff of it until we was tuckered out. Then, when we went back, with the hunger and the wildness out of us, we could watch the snow fall and feel warm inside." He inclined his head. "You remember that, feeling that, John?"

"I remember all of it, Tom. The hunger and the wildness and all of it."

Tom straightened again in his chair. "Young is the time for snow. It's the only time you can give it what it asks of you. For later, when we was men, and the first snow come, the same urging was still with us. But a grown man can't roll in the white stuff of it. He can't heave snowballs, or shout, or carry on in any way. He must sit and watch it, and get up and pace the room, and feel that he must be about something, but what that something is, he doesn't know."

Tom fell silent. The wood in the stove rustled as it settled deeper into the grate, and the flame was beginning to wane. It danced less often now. A silence crept over the saloon and min-gled with the gloom until the two were one, and silence lived and breathed with gloom.

Tom did not move when the door to the saloon opened, and a man, his shoulders hunched from walking in the storm, came in. He carried a black dinner pail in his hand, and he set it down on the bar before shaking the snow from his coat.

The barkeeper rose from his stool and poured out a tumbler of whiskey. They exchanged low words of greeting, and the man started to raise the tumbler to his lips. But as he did, he chanced to look towards the back of the room. He lowered the drink and spoke to the barkeeper.

He waited as the barkeeper moved slowly back and stopped beside the old man's chair.

"Tom . . ."

The old man started and then turned stiffly, confusion shining in his eyes.

"Uh . . . what, Iver?" Then he saw the barkeeper. "Oh, it's you, Billy."

The barkeeper was silent for an instant. His foot shuffled on the floor, self-consciously, as a child in the presence of his elders. But when he spoke, his voice was almost harsh, as though he were angry with himself. "Tom, do you want a drink? Joe Lindsey's boy wants to buy you a drink."

Tom shook his head. "No, thank ya, Billy. You tell him thank ya, anyway. I'm not feeling right up tonight. You tell him thank ya, anyway, Billy."

Even after the barkeeper had gone, Tom was still smiling. "That was nice of the boy, wasn't it? He's a good boy, he is. A boy Joe would be proud of, to see the way he turned out, a good family man and all."

The wood in the grate slipped again with a groan and settled into the ashes. The flame flickered brightly once more, and then died. The coals glowed red through the chinks for an instant, but the glow faded, and the chinks became dark. The fire was almost out, and Tom listened for the final rustle of its going. It came, soft and breathless, like a sigh out of the snow. The silence returned to the gloom.

The hand that touched Tom on the shoulder was gloved, and when he turned, the barkeeper stood there, already wrapped in his coat.

"Time to go, Tom. Got to close her up."

The old man rose from the chair. "All right, Billy. All right." He moved towards the rack and pulled down the black hat and coat, then walked with the barkeeper to the front of the saloon. As he walked, he pulled on the coat and buttoned it.

"Snow's stopped, Tom."

The old man squinted through the pane of the big door. "Why, it has at that. The first snow's come and gone, and now, the winter will come." He pulled the shapeless black hat over his gray head, then stopped as if remembering something, and peered quickly towards the back of the room.

But as he turned, the barkeeper pulled the single light string, and darkness, becoming cold now, fell over the saloon. The barkeeper opened the door and followed the old man out, flipping the lever to the lock as he went.

They stood together on the walk for a moment, and then the old man murmured, "Good night, Billy."

"Good night, Tom. Good night."

The barkeeper watched until the old man had moved through the arc of light from the street lamp, and he could no longer distinguish his figure from the darkness.

Then he turned, and plunging his gloved hands into the deep pockets of his coat, he made his own way home, kicking angrily at the snow as he went.

# WESTERN LITERATURE SERIES

Western Trails: A Collection
of Short Stories by Mary Austin
  *selected and edited by*
  *Melody Graulich*

Cactus Thorn
  *by Mary Austin*

Dan De Quille, the Washoe Giant:
A Biography and Anthology
  *prepared by Richard A. Dwyer and*
  *Richard E. Lingenfelter*

Desert Wood: An Anthology of
Nevada Poets
  *edited by Shaun T. Griffin*

The City of Trembling Leaves
  *by Walter Van Tilburg Clark*

Many Californias: Literature from the
Golden State
  *edited by Gerald W. Haslam*

The Authentic Death of Hendry Jones
  *by Charles Neider*

First Horses: Stories of the New West
  *by Robert Franklin Gish*

Torn by Light: Selected Poems
  *by Joanne de Longchamps*

Swimming Man Burning
  *by Terrence A. Kilpatrick*

The Temptations of St. Ed
and Brother S
  *by Frank Bergon*

The Other California: The Great
Central Valley in Life and Letters
  *by Gerald W. Haslam*

The Track of the Cat
  *by Walter Van Tilburg Clark*

Condor Dreams and Other Fictions
  *by Gerald W. Haslam*

A Lean Year and Other Stories
  *by Robert Laxalt*